The Scratch on the Ming Vase

A Nicki Haddon
Mystery

The Scratch on the Ming Vase

CAROLINE STELLINGS

Second Story Press

Library and Archives Canada Cataloguing in Publication

Stellings, Caroline, 1961-
The scratch on the Ming vase / by Caroline Stellings.

Issued also in an electronic format.
ISBN 978-1-926920-91-7

I. Title.

PS8587.T4448S37 2012   jC813'.6   C2012-904017-7

*Second Story Press gratefully acknowledges the support of the Ontario Arts Council
and the Canada Council for the Arts for our publishing program. We acknowledge
the financial support of the Government of Canada through the Canada Book Fund.*

ONTARIO ARTS COUNCIL
CONSEIL DES ARTS DE L'ONTARIO

Canada Council   Conseil des Art
for the Arts   du Canada

Published by
SECOND STORY PRESS
20 Maud Street, Suite 401
Toronto, ON M5V 2M5
www.secondstorypress.ca

The Scratch on the Ming Vase

Prologue
Honolulu, Hawaii, 1901

On a balmy night in the middle of August, an assassin skims through the darkened streets of Chinatown. The claptrap restaurants and laundries are sprawled over a dozen blocks, a maze of crazy alleys with no beginning and no end. His cotton shirt is threadbare, and he's sweaty from the thick heat that even the strongest Kona trade wind can't blow out of town. The shops on Maunakea Street are long-since closed for the night, but the oily cooking smells linger, mixing with salty Pacific air and the pungent smoke from opium dens.

He looks up to the one window where a sliver of light sneaks out from behind a blind and rests on the fringe of a coconut palm. He feels his front pocket for a pack of cigarettes and his back one for a six-inch knife. It isn't long before his contact arrives and they lock eyes.

Their whispered conversation, in a Cantonese dialect, lasts only a few seconds. There's a yellow ring around the perigee moon, and it breaks their stare.

The assassin is told to get it right the first time.

He grabs a cardboard box out of his contact's arms, opens the flaps, and peers inside. A faint smile flickers at the corners of his mouth. The Ming vase in there is worth more greenbacks then he could hope to make in ten lifetimes. And it isn't his life that's about to end. It's Sun Yat-sen's.

The Manchu regime has a price on Sun's head that's too high for any man to resist. Someone has to stop the reformer from changing four thousand years of rule in China. Someone's got to shut him up.

The contact waits behind a palm tree while the killer climbs the wooden stairs. They creak, so he stops for a minute, then takes two at a time. He presses his ear against the wall to hear Sun Yat-sen rallying his recruits. Then he smiles again and kicks open the door.

The knife hits Sun's collarbone, and he survives to tell the tale.

The assassin does time for attempted murder.

He names his contact.

The vase winds up in a vault at the police station on Bethel Street.

Chapter One

Rain drenched the streets of Toronto's Chinatown. Streaming off roofs and through gutters, then gushing into the sewers, it carried with it the dust of one of the hottest summers on record. The fruit stands and fish markets and herb shops stayed open for business under canopies, their owners oblivious to both the heat and the rain.

Nicki arrived in Toronto in the evening; she caught a bus from the airport, then a subway to Chinatown. She was used to the city in July and the kind of humidity that sticks to you like a second skin. In some ways, she preferred it to Honolulu. No turquoise ocean lapped at her door, and no plumeria-scented breeze wafted by, but whenever she landed in Toronto, it felt like home.

The sixteen-year-old pulled a rumpled paper from her

duffel bag and checked the address she'd scrawled down while still in the Pineapple State. She was close now, closer than ever to her dream of working with David Kahana. A native Hawaiian, and one of the most highly respected martial artists in the world, he had come to Toronto for the summer to train elite athletes.

Nicki ran the last block, stopping once to shake off the rain and ask for directions to the Fire Dragon Academy.

An old Chinese woman pointed across the street, and Nicki spotted it. It was modest: a couple of rooms on the second floor over a tavern full of drunks, but it looked like heaven to her. She gazed up at it and smiled, glad to see that the lights were still on.

Good, she thought. *We can work out a schedule right away.*

She climbed a narrow staircase that had spent the last two decades as a canvas for street artists. At the top, where the concrete ended and a dirty carpet began, a smudge caught her eye—blood red and in the shape of a shoe.

Looks like paint, she told herself. She knew it wasn't. And it wasn't graffiti red—too dark for that.

Blood. It was blood. Fresh blood. And someone had tracked it out of the Fire Dragon Academy.

Maybe it's from a nosebleed. She'd had a few of those herself, when the sparring got too vigorous. *Or maybe the students have been working with swords.*

The rationalizations didn't work. Her pulse quickened.

The door swung open when she touched it.

When she passed the threshold, a nail sticking out of the

woodwork snagged her pant leg. She pulled herself loose, then stepped inside.

"Hello," she mumbled. "Master Kahana?"

The only replies came from a car horn at street level and a guy yelling at his girlfriend in the bar.

A desk in the middle of the room was covered with files, empty coffee cups, business cards, martial arts magazines, and manuals. Nicki followed the footprints past the desk; they came from the training room. Halfway in, a trail of red accompanied the footprints to the door of a storage area.

She opened it.

Inside lay David Kahana, face down in a pool of blood.

"Master?" gasped Nicki.

His head moved.

"Nicki…"

"Yes, it's me."

"The…Ming…" Kahana was trying to tell her something.

"I can't hear you."

"The vase," he murmured. "Get the vase…no police…"

"Vase?"

"Everything…is up to you."

Chapter Two

The wailing drew closer and closer until Nicki's ears burned. Lights—whirling, flashing, pulsing lights—bounced off the building. Tires screeched, sirens blared, and people hollered.

Nicki's cell phone was still in her hand, and the 911 operator was slamming her with questions when the rescue team arrived.

Minutes. It took only minutes. There was nothing she could do with a wound like that, and she knew it. *Thank goodness they got here so fast.*

They took Kahana out in a stretcher. He wasn't dead. Not yet, anyway. The paramedics wouldn't be working so hard if he were.

Nicki's heart pounded. She sank onto a bench in the hallway. Inches from her foot, not far from the door to the academy and spattered with blood, lay a small filing card.

She examined it carefully; it had yellowed with time, and what was once black ink had faded to dull gray. It read:

Property of the Honolulu Police Department, 842 Bethel Street. Seized August 15, 1901, during attempted murder of Sun Yat-Sen. File No. 15738B

That's the old station downtown in the historic district, she thought.

She slipped the card into her bag as a female officer strode through the door.

"Miss," said the officer, "I'll take you to the hospital."

"I'm all right."

"Let's have a physician confirm that." The officer took Nicki to the hospital in a cruiser, left her in the emergency room, and told her she'd be back to ask some questions. "Stick around," was how she put it.

A young hospital volunteer slid into the seat next to Nicki and handed her a coffee. Her name tag read *Margo Bloom*.

"I thought you could use this," she said. She was about the same age as Nicki, with an open and happy face and curly, brown hair. She wore a pink uniform with matching running shoes and a pink-and-white striped vest.

Horrible color, thought Nicki. "Do they know anything at all about Mr. Kahana's condition?" she asked. She couldn't stop her hand from shaking, and half the coffee hit the floor.

The volunteer mopped it up with a wad of tissues.

"All I know is that they took him to intensive care. And even if I knew, I wouldn't be allowed to tell you anything. I'm just a volunteer." She extended her hand. "I'm Margo Bloom, by the way."

"There's nothing you can tell me?"

"I might get away with the weather."

Nicki pulled out her wallet. "What do I owe you for the coffee?"

"Oh, that's okay. Don't worry about it." She removed the lid from her own cup. "I hope you like cream and sugar." Margo covered a yawn with the lid.

"I do," said Nicki, although she never touched the stuff.

The girl yawned again. "Sorry. I've been trying to fit in my hours here at night."

"After school?" asked Nicki.

Margo nodded. "And work. I plan on going to nursing school next year—if I can stay awake long enough to pass calculus. Plus, I'm dieting. I want to look good in my new disco dress. Well, it will be mine if it goes on sale."

"Disco? Really?"

"There's a retro night at the club where my friends and I go," said the girl. "The university students hang out there, but you can get in if you're sixteen." She smiled. "Oh, you should see this dress. The clerk told me the store owner is reducing a lot of items next week, so I'm keeping my fingers crossed."

"Here, I want to pay for the coffee," said Nicki, handing her a five-dollar bill.

"No, it's okay." Margo tossed back her java like she'd found ice water after a week in the Sahara. "My parents have a deli around the corner. Business isn't what it used to be, but I still manage to smile my way to the odd tip."

Margo glanced at Nicki's shoes and sweats. They were splattered with mud. One pant leg was torn where the nail had caught it. "Do you have a place to stay tonight?" she asked.

She thinks I'm homeless, thought Nicki. "Listen, Margo—"

"Oh, you don't have to explain anything. I understand how it is. Times are tough for everybody." She patted Nicki's wrist.

"I appreciate your concern," said Nicki. "But—"

A nurse interrupted.

"Margo, we need some help in the geriatric ward."

Margo stood up. "Nice to meet you," she said. "I hope your friend gets better." She headed for the elevator.

Nicki dumped the coffee down the drain of a water fountain, then made her way to the intensive care unit.

She combed the halls until she found David Kahana— barely alive and being wheeled into surgery.

"You'll have to get out of the way." A blood-soaked nurse shouldered Nicki to the side.

The door to the operating room slammed shut.

Chapter Three

Nicki paced the floors. An hour later, the officer returned and found her in the foyer. "Hasn't anyone checked you over yet?" she asked, taking Nicki by the arm. One look at the crowd of people slumped against walls and the officer had her answer. "I guess you want to go home." She headed to the main desk and found a nurse who took thirty seconds to check Nicki's blood pressure and determine she wasn't in shock.

"It's okay, I'm fine," said Nicki. "I just want to know who tried to kill Mr. Kahana." She looked at the officer. "Do you have any leads at all?"

"I didn't come here to answer questions, I came to ask them." The officer took a pad out of her jacket and dug through her pockets to find a pen. "What can you tell me about Mr. Kabbana?"

"Kahana. I met him in Honolulu and planned on taking classes with him this summer."

"Are you…Hawaiian? I thought you were—"

"Chinese? You thought right."

★ ★ ★

Nicki dashed from the hospital lobby and across the parking lot.

"Thanks for coming," she said, jumping into the frontseat of the luxury sedan. "Hope you don't mind if I ride up front. I can't stand the backseat." She threw her bag onto the floor. "You must be our new butler. I'm glad to finally meet you, Fenwick."

"Very pleased to meet you, Miss," replied the gray-haired man. "But are you sure that you should—?"

"Be in the front? Who's going to know?"

The butler nodded and smiled. "I would know you any-where from your portrait, Miss."

"Oh, right, the portrait," mumbled the teenager. She rolled her eyes. "So you're from England?"

"Yes, Miss. From Milchester."

"Milchester?"

"A little town, southeast of London." The rain splashed in the window, so he closed it tight. "My sister and I have a cottage there."

"You must be used to weather like this," said Nicki. "Every time I compete in London, it rains." She reached inside her bag for a water bottle and chugged some back. "What's your real name, Fenwick? And please, you don't have to call me Miss."

"Willard Huntington Wright, Miss...uh, Nicki. But Mrs. Haddon insists—"

"I know—that you're Fenwick. Our butlers are all Fenwicks. Even our Filipino butler in Manila is Fenwick."

"I'm sorry, I didn't realize you had arrived. I would have picked you up at the airport." He turned off the motor.

"I decided to take an earlier flight at the last minute," said Nicki. She fanned herself with her hand.

"Are you all right? If you don't mind my saying, you look a bit, well, uh..."

"I went to Chinatown tonight to meet with David Kahana. He's a Grand Master of kung fu and one of the best martial artists in the world," Nicki explained. "Fenwick, someone put a sword through his back tonight, and I don't know if he's going to survive."

The color left the butler's face.

Fenwick rubbed his knuckles nervously. Nicki noticed that part of the first finger on his right hand was missing. "I wish I had known you were back," he said. "Why didn't you wait and fly with your mother?"

"I hate private jets. Anyway, she wanted to stay in Honolulu for a few more days."

"And your father?"

"He's in Paris, I think." The Haddons owned an international chain of luxury hotels and resorts. Their Toronto home, a mansion on the Bridle Path, was cared for by Fenwick and a small household staff.

Nicki took another sip of water. "I was going to call you."

"I don't think your parents would like you to be on the streets alone."

"I can look after myself."

"Yes, I suppose you can," Fenwick admitted. "The cook tells me you're a silver medalist in kung fu."

"Gold."

"Your parents must be terribly proud, Miss."

She shrugged her shoulders. "I don't know," she said. "Maybe." She put her thumb over the mouth of the bottle and shook it until it fizzed. "I was hoping one of them could have been there to see my wushu team compete last week. We won in both the bare-handed and sword competitions. But they're always busy. Always."

Fenwick wiped condensation off the window with his handkerchief. "That must be difficult for you, Miss."

Nicki had no response.

"They're good people, the Haddons," offered Fenwick.

"Oh, yes," said Nicki. "And I'm grateful for everything. It's just that—"

"They haven't always been there for you. I understand."

Nicki turned in her seat to face the butler. "Were you adopted?"

"No, Miss. But my parents did leave my sister and me to be raised by an uncle." He lowered his gaze. "It wasn't an easy time for us."

"I'm sorry," said the girl. *I like Fenwick*, she thought. *I think I can trust him.*

The two of them sat quietly for a minute.

"Did the cook tell you the rest of my life story?" asked Nicki.

Fenwick nodded.

"Guangdong province," she said. "The last place you'd choose to be born, right?" The butler nodded again. "I like to think my birth parents had no choice. Maybe it was thanks to China's one-child policy, I don't know. But leaving me in a box on the side of a busy street? One careless driver and I'd have been roadkill."

Fenwick shook his head in disbelief. "It's always the baby girls who are abandoned," he said.

"But why leave *this* with me?" She reached for a charm that was dangling on a chain around her neck. "This is the Chinese character for good luck." She let go of it. "Why bother if you're going to leave somebody to die?"

Fenwick had no answer.

"Well, anyway," she said, "that's how Fu Yin became Nicki Haddon."

"Fu Yin?"

"Every baby in the orphanage gets the surname Fu. My given name was Yin. My parents—well, the Haddons— changed it to Nicki."

They stared out the windshield. Then the butler spoke up.

"Ever wonder about them?"

"Sometimes."

"Have you tried to find them?"

"No." Nicki leaned back in her seat. "Wouldn't know where to start."

There was a pause.

"May I take you home now?" asked Fenwick.

"Not yet." She buried her face in her hands and sighed. "I don't know what to do."

"About what, Miss?"

"I can't dump this on you—I mean, I've only known you for a few minutes." She took a deep breath. "But I feel I can trust you. My parents think a lot of you, that's for sure."

"Of course you can trust me."

"Master Kahana insisted that I find a Ming vase."

"A Ming vase? How will you do that?" asked the butler.

"I don't know. But I've got to start somewhere."

The martial arts academy swarmed with crime-scene investigators. Fenwick stopped when he saw the yellow tape across the door. Nicki ducked underneath.

"I'll be back in a minute," she told him.

She darted upstairs.

A senior officer noticed her immediately.

"What do you think you're doing?" he shouted.

"I'm looking for something…I left behind," she said.

"Look, Miss," said the cop, "this is a crime scene. You'll have to leave."

The female officer who had accompanied Nicki to the hospital stepped forward. "This is the girl who found the victim," she offered.

"I'll only be a minute." Nicki's eyes scoured the room.

"You'll go now," said the cop. He turned to the female officer. "Get her out of here."

"Okay, I'm leaving," said Nicki.

The female officer escorted her downstairs.

Nicki went to find Fenwick, but a conversation between two officers stirred her curiosity. Their voices were barely audible over the sounds from the street. She listened intently.

"The RCMP is going to be handling the investigation," said one of them. "Once we're finished here."

"The Royal Canadian Mounted Police? Why?"

"David Kahana isn't just a kung fu expert," replied the officer. "He's a United States Secret Service agent."

Chapter Four

"You had no idea?" asked Fenwick.

"No, not really," said Nicki, as the limo pulled through the wrought-iron gates and onto the driveway of the Bridle Path mansion. "I met the Grand Master once at an event in Honolulu. He watched me compete; about a month later, he asked me if I wanted to train with him in Toronto. I jumped at the chance, believe me." Nicki released her seat belt. "Someone said he worked as a bodyguard for the president while he was vacationing in Hawaii."

"And that's why the Royal Canadian Mounted Police have been called in?" asked Fenwick. By the time he got out of the car and came around to open the door for Nicki, she was already out and halfway across the lawn. She waited by the tennis court for him to pull the car into the garage.

"I guess. Makes sense if he's involved with the intelligence program," said Nicki. "And I can see why he would be. He's an authority in surgical strike techniques. He's very close to holding the highest title that anyone can achieve—Supreme Grand Master—and he's ranked as a tenth degree black belt."

"I see," said the butler.

"He could take out three or four men with one arm tied behind his back." Nicki picked up a stray ball and fired it into the court. "Whoever tried to kill him tonight must have taken him completely by surprise. It's the only way the fiend could have done this."

"And what about you?" asked Fenwick.

"What about me?"

"How many men could you take out with an arm tied behind your back?"

Nicki grinned. "I don't know. Maybe two?"

★ ★ ★

By the time the butler called her for breakfast, Nicki had been gone for hours. After an early morning run through the trails of the Don River Valley, followed by a quick shower, she headed for the hospital.

"Is there any change in Mr. Kahana's condition?" she asked the nurse in charge.

"Are you a family member?"

"I'm a close friend. Is there anything you can tell me?"

She leaned over the reception desk. "Does the surgeon expect him to live?"

"Hi there," said a voice from behind a cart of books and videos. It was Margo Bloom. She smiled at Nicki while the nurse checked the file.

"I thought you worked at night," said Nicki.

"I'm here whenever they need me."

"How is Grand Master Kahana?" Nicki bit her bottom lip.

"Grand Master?"

"He's a kung fu expert."

"He is?" Margo looked at Nicki. "Do you know martial arts?"

"Yes."

"Wow!" said Margo. "I'd like to find a class in that one day. My dad's always after me to take self-defense. Are you just learning?"

The nurse interrupted.

"David Kahana is in a comatose state," she said, with no expression in either her voice or her face. "That's all I can tell you."

Nicki sat down in the lounge, and Margo joined her.

"People can come out of comas," offered the girl. "And Mr. Kahana must be very fit, right?"

Nicki nodded her head. "What about his personal effects?" she asked. "Did he have anything with him when he arrived? Any notes? Anything?"

"I think the police took everything," said Margo. "But I'm not supposed to say anything—"

"Except the weather." Nicki turned in her seat. "You must have seen what they took away."

"No, the only thing I saw was a key card. One of the nurses found it and gave it to the police."

"A key card? For a hotel?" asked Nicki.

"Yes, that's right."

"For which hotel? Did you get a look at it?"

"I sure did," said Margo. "It was for Haddon Heights. You know the place. It's right beside our deli." A nurse walked by and gave Margo a steely look. Margo got up and wheeled her cart out of the lounge. "The Haddons own the building our deli is in."

"Really?" Nicki followed her down the hall. "Listen, Margo, I've been wanting—"

"Yes, really. And they're filthy rich. Filthy stinking rich. Yet they raise our rent every chance they get. I think they want to drive my parents out of business so they can tear down the deli."

"Margo—"

"They'll put in a parking lot or something. They won't worry about us." She straightened a stack of books that had fallen over. "Sorry, what did you say?"

"Nothing. I've got to go."

"Why don't you come with me to the dance on Friday night? You'd love it!"

"Thanks, but—"

"Oh, come on."

"Maybe some other time." Nicki walked away.

"Hey," said Margo, "what's your name, anyway?" She

caught up with Nicki. "I hope you don't think I'm nosy. I just… well, I don't know what to call you."

Nicki stopped abruptly, turned around, and looked Margo in the eye.

"Yin," she said. "Fu Yin."

Chapter Five

Nicki stood in front of Haddon Heights hotel and gazed up at the cascade of plate glass windows that reached so high into the sky even the clouds could see their reflection. Taxis pulled up in front, people came and went, streetcars shuttled by, and men and women in suits filed into the canopied outdoor restaurant to order tall drinks in iced glasses.

Next door, outside Bloom's Deli, two men on a picnic table bench drank coffee out of chipped mugs and ate blintzes and bagels and argued over exactly how thin pastrami should be sliced. A woman came out, filled up their cups, and handed them each a creamer and a paper envelope of sugar.

She must be Margo's mom, thought Nicki.

They laughed about something, then the woman shuffled back inside. She stopped at the door to adjust a sign that was propped in the front window. It read *Same Great Menu. New Prices.*

Nicki headed for the hotel lobby.

"Excuse me," said the doorman. "Are you a guest?"

"No."

"You'll need proper attire for the dining room."

Nicki pushed past him and through the revolving door.

"Can you tell me what room Mr. David Kahana is staying in?" she asked the receptionist.

"I'm sorry," the woman replied curtly, "I can't give out that information." She turned her back to Nicki.

"Fine."

Nicki headed down the first corridor and found a bellhop carrying some luggage to the service elevator.

"Wow," said Nicki, "I'll be glad when things are back to normal on my floor. The whole thing makes me uneasy."

"What makes you uneasy?"

"The attempted murder of that hotel guest."

"Oh, right," the bellhop said.

Nicki reached into her pocket. "Darn! I've left my key card upstairs. You aren't going to my floor by any chance, are you?"

"The eighth? No, I'm not," he replied. "But they can help you at the main desk."

Nicki thanked him and hurried back to the lobby.

Silver chandeliers hung like earrings from the ceiling, and every stick of furniture flaunted velvet cushions. Even the elevators had attitude—gold doors with platinum fittings and original paintings on the walls. The uniformed elevator operator beckoned her inside with white gloves.

She took the stairs.

A police guard stood outside room 813.

Nicki approached him.

"Mr. Kahana asked me to retrieve something for him."

"You can't enter the room. I'm sorry."

"He's in intensive care. I have to—"

"Not even staff members can enter this room," he said. "Not until the forensics team gets here and gives the all clear."

Staff members. That gave Nicki an idea, and she headed back downstairs.

She assumed the manager's office wouldn't be far from her mother's, near the front desk. She was right; the black oak door displayed a brass sign that read *Trent Newman, Manager*. The door was slightly ajar, so she rapped on it and walked in.

The manager swung around in his chair. He had thick brown hair and a mustache that grew over the corner of his mouth. His face was sunburned, his eyes yellowish-gray.

"What is it?" he asked.

"I'm here to apply for a job," said Nicki.

"In the restaurant? I don't need any waitresses."

"No. Housekeeping."

He pointed to a stack of applications sitting on a bureau near the door.

"Blue form," he said. "Make it quick, will you?"

Nicki sat on the floor in the hallway and filled it out, complete with false address, false references, and false employment history. She went back into the office and handed it to Newman.

"Fu Yin. And you've just moved here?"

"Yes."

"From where?"

"Buffalo."

While he scanned the form, she glanced at the photos on his desk. In one of them, he was standing next to an older woman in the front yard of a small, wood-frame bungalow, surrounded by flowering hibiscus plants. He had no mustache then. In the distant background was Diamond Head, the distinctive landmark near Waikiki.

Oh, no. He's from Hawaii!

She felt a slight moment of panic and then she thought about it.

He won't recognize me.

She looked at the photograph again, trying to figure out where in Honolulu it was taken.

That's out in the suburbs. Looks like Kaimuki.

Newman followed her gaze to the photograph. "My mother," he mumbled. He picked up the application form. "What about your Social Insurance Number?" he said. "You say it's forthcoming. What's that supposed to mean?"

"The employment office said it might take a couple of weeks."

"When they say two weeks, they mean two months." He tugged at his mustache. "I can wait for it if you want to work for me. God knows I need housekeepers. But I can't pay you until I have the number. It's up to you."

"Okay."

"Can you handle a cleaning position?" he asked. "You don't look very strong. What are you, five feet tall?"

"Five two," she replied. "And yes, I can handle it."

"I hope so."

His cell phone rang.

He pulled it out of a brown briefcase sitting on the floor next to his feet.

"Just a minute," he said to the person who had called, then to Nicki, "Report to the head of housekeeping."

"Thank you," she said.

Newman didn't reply.

Nicki pulled the door behind her, but didn't let it click shut.

"Aloha, Kimo," said Newman, leaning back in his chair.

Kimo must be Hawaiian. She peeked through the crack.

Newman threw both his feet up on the desk and put one arm behind his head.

"Arrested any chicken thieves lately?" Newman laughed.

And Kimo must be a cop.

Chapter Six

Nicki was in the den going through her mother's desk when Fenwick came in, feather duster in hand.

"What are you doing, Miss Nicki?"

"I need my mother's pass key for Haddon Heights, and I need the override tool. I have to bypass the security system, and I've got to be able to open a safe." She searched the drawers until she found them.

"I don't understand, Miss."

"I don't have much time. I've got to be back at the hotel in less than an hour." She looked at her watch. "I've taken a job there."

"You've done what?"

"It's the only way, Fenwick. I've got to find that vase for Mr. Kahana. And Haddon Heights is where he was staying."

"Just tell the manager who you are, Nicki, and he'll help you, I'm sure."

"I doubt it. If I reveal my identity, everyone will clam up and watch my every move. That's the last thing I need right now."

"But there's a murderer out there, Miss Nicki. How do you know—"

"I don't know." She turned to leave. "Fenwick, you've got to promise me that you won't say a word to anyone. Please."

★ ★ ★

Nicki picked up a mop and pail and followed Dolores and Ellen into the service elevator.

"You'll be dead on your feet for the first week or two, then you'll get used to it. Once the blisters heal." Dolores pulled a compact out of her pocket and checked her face. "Always look your best, Yin," she added. "There are lots of millionaires in this place, and plenty of them are single. That's how I'm going to escape one day. On a yacht. Hopefully before I'm thirty."

"You turned thirty last year, didn't you?" Ellen tapped her fingernails against the wringer bucket. "Only way out of here before you're sixty-five is in an ambulance. Or a coffin."

Dolores glanced at Nicki.

"You're too young for this. You should try for something better. If I had it to do all over, I'd become an actress or a hair-dresser or something. Something glamorous." She pulled out a pair of rubber gloves and snapped them on. "So where do we start, girls?"

"How about the eighth floor?" said Nicki.

"Sounds good," said Ellen. "That way I can talk to that handsome police guard."

"Someone tried to murder the man who was staying in 813," Dolores told Nicki. She felt around in her pocket, then handed the girl a staff keycard. "This will work on any door in the hotel, but remember, every time you use it, it's recorded on the computer downstairs. The room number, the time, and the fact that it was your card." She smirked. "That way, if a guest can't find her pearl necklace, they'll have somebody to blame."

The service elevator opened, and they lifted the cleaning cart out and started down the hall. Ellen smiled at the policeman when they passed room 813.

They walked to the far end of the corridor and pushed open the door to a recently vacated suite. "Looks like they've been having some fun in here." Dolores tossed a load of clean linens onto the bed.

Toppled wine and liquor bottles oozed out their dregs onto the rug, half-eaten plates of shrimp and lobster slopped over the dresser, and honey from the breakfast tray coated the TV remote. The bathroom was even worse.

Slobs, she thought.

"Start with the bed," said Ellen. "I'll face the bathroom."

Nicki threw off the quilt, stripped the bed down, and reached for the fresh sheets. She threw one over the bed and started to jam the edges under the mattress.

"What the heck are you doing?" Dolores leaned her dust mop against the wall and called Ellen out of the bathroom.

"Will you look at this? The girl has never made a bed in her life!"

Ellen laughed. "Here's how it's done," she said, starting with a fitted sheet and smoothing it out from the middle to each end. "Everything has to be tight as a drum, and remember that the flat sheet always goes good side down, so when you fold it back—and it must be exactly one-third of the bed—the right side will face up."

"Got it," said Nicki.

"Oh Yin," said Dolores. "Don't forget the chocolate on the pillow."

★　★　★

Dolores checked out the room. "Not bad, not bad at all. You catch on fast," she said. "We're going on our break now, Yin. Take fifteen."

"You can join us if you want," said Ellen. The staff lunch-room is in the basement, next to the laundry."

Dolores made a face. "The vending machine spits out stale sandwiches and warm juice, but if you give it a swift kick, it returns your coins."

"Not mine," said Ellen.

"You're not lucky like me."

"Right, Dolores."

"Thanks, but I don't want anything right now. I'll see you later," said Nicki.

She watched from the end of the hall as the two women

headed for the elevator. Ellen stopped to chat with the cop and Dolores joined her. This was Nicki's chance and she took it.

I just hope Newman isn't watching the surveillance camera.

Dragging a mop and pail, she shot up the hall to room 813.

"I heard a scream," she told the guard at the door. "A terrible scream from across the atrium. Someone's in trouble!" The cop dashed down the corridor, then headed toward the atrium.

Ellen and Dolores ran behind him.

"Come on, Yin!" they hollered.

Nicki knocked her pail over with her foot. "Oh, no!" she cried. "You two go. Hurry! I'll be right there."

Once they were out of sight, Nicki pulled out her mother's universal passkey, rammed it into the slot, grabbed her mop and pail, and quickly shut the door behind her.

She went straight to the in-room safe.

The vase has to be in there. Her mind raced as she pulled out the override tool.

It was!

Standing alone in the middle of that cold metal safe was the most exquisite piece of porcelain she had ever seen. But there was no time to admire it now. Nicki grabbed a thick towel from the bathroom, wrapped it around the vase, and carefully placed it in the bottom of her pail. Then she opened the door a crack and peered down the hall.

Good. I still have a bit of time.

She riffled through Kahana's shirts in the chest of drawers.

There's got to be a clue here someplace. Something to lead me to the creep who stabbed Master Kahana.

Next she tried the closet.

It was empty except for a couple of light jackets. She went through the pockets, but there was only a package of gum and a slip of paper. On it Kahana had written a phone number and a name: Robert A-G. Nicki shoved it into her pocket.

Sensing her time was up, she crept out the door, just as the cop was coming down the hall. Wheeling her mop and pail to the service elevator, she took a deep breath and prayed that he didn't see her get on.

He didn't.

But Trent Newman did. When the doors opened, he was standing in the elevator.

Chapter Seven

"What the devil are you doing?" Newman had a chunk of Spam in his hand. No bun, no mustard, just Spam. Neat.

Now I know he's a kama'aina, thought Nicki. *Nobody can stomach Spam like a born-and-bred Hawaiian. There isn't a restaurant in Honolulu that doesn't serve it.*

"You're supposed to be cleaning with your team! Why aren't you?"

Nicki shrugged. Then she noticed that the towel had shifted and part of the vase was exposed. She draped her mop over it in an attempt to conceal it from Newman.

It felt like the longest elevator ride of her life.

"Find your team and don't go off on your own, do you hear me?" declared Newman. "Any more missteps and you're history."

Newman stuffed the meat into his mouth, holding it between his teeth so it didn't fall out, then stomped through the door when the elevator finally came to a stop.

Nicki hurried to her mother's office on the main floor. When no one was looking, she slipped inside and found a place to hide the vase. Then she called home.

"I need your help, Fenwick. And I need it now."

"My help, Miss?"

"I've got the vase."

"You found it?"

"I'll explain later. Right now it's hidden in my mother's office at the hotel, but I've got to get it out of here. I'll be working on one of the floors, but I'll keep my eye out for you every chance I get. Bring a suitcase, Fenwick. And try to look like one of the guests."

"I'll try."

"Oh, and Fenwick?" Out of her pocket Nicki pulled the slip of paper she'd found in room 813. "Can you do a reverse phone check for me?"

Nicki finished work at seven. Before she left, she returned to the eighth floor, stood with her back against the wall and peered around the corner toward 813. The forensics team was inside, poking into every corner. Newman stood outside the room, hands folded in front, a vacant look on his face.

After a few minutes, a detective came out.

"We're almost finished in there, Mr. Newman," he said.

Investigators shuffled past; they didn't appear to be carrying anything from the room.

"Didn't they find anything?" demanded Newman.

"I can't tell you that," answered the detective.

"Mr. Kahana informed me that he required a room with a safe," said Newman. "I believe he must have deposited something valuable in there." His face went red. "I need to know for insurance purposes. If there's going to be a claim—"

"No, sir," said the detective. "There was nothing in the safe."

"What?" Newman craned his neck to look inside, but the detective pulled the door shut. "But I'm sure—"

"Sure of what?"

"Well, Mr. Kahana specifically asked me about the safe. I'm sure he must have—"

"I'm sorry, sir," said the detective. "You'll have your room back shortly."

"Good!" snapped Newman, and he stormed down the hall.

Nicki ducked into a closet. While Newman hammered the elevator button with his fist, she took the stairs to the ground floor and headed outside.

On her way to the hospital she passed Bloom's Deli, just as Margo came out the door.

"Yin!" Margo called. "Come on over! Do you like corned beef?"

Before Nicki could explain she was vegetarian, Margo had already set her a place at the picnic table and was bringing out food by the boatloads. "Not too busy tonight, so we've got tons of leftovers."

"Margo," said Nicki, "I'm not a meat eater myself, so I—"

"No problem. Have a bagel and cream cheese. And rye bread. And pickles. And lox—do you eat fish? And coffee!"

She sure loves her coffee, thought Nicki.

"Thanks, I guess I am pretty hungry." Nicki tossed back two bagels and half a dozen pickles.

Margo smiled. "You like pickles."

"I love pickles," admitted Nicki, helping herself to another. "And these are the best I've ever eaten." She scrunched up her napkin and let it drop into the middle of the empty plate. "I must have built up an appetite; I've been cleaning rooms at the hotel all day."

"You got a job? Hey, that's great!"

Ira and Ruthie Bloom, Margo's parents, brought out sticky buns and soup and more coffee.

"This is my new friend, Yin," said Margo. "And these are my parents." She made a sweeping motion with her left hand while reaching for a bun with her right.

Margo's dad took a place on the bench.

"You girls care to join me in a bowl of soup?"

"I don't think there's room for all three of you in there," quipped Ruthie, making Margo laugh.

"Sit down, Mom."

"There are still some customers to serve."

"You can never have too many customers," said Ira. "In

the old days, you could, but no more. I'm telling you…what's your name again?"

"Yin."

"I'm telling you, Yin, this health food craze is going to put me out of business. Nobody wants pastrami, nobody wants kreplach, nobody wants knishes. They act like anything with a bit of *schmaltz* will kill them on the spot. My grandfather in Brooklyn lived until he was ninety-eight, and he ate nothing but schmaltz. And cream soda."

"Schmaltz?" asked Nicki.

"Fat," Margo managed to squeeze in before Ira was off again.

"All this nonsense about health," cried Ira. "You know what it is, girls? You know what it is?" He swallowed a big spoonful of soup. "*Bupkis!* That's what it is!"

"Bupkis?" asked Nicki.

"That means nonsense," said Margo. "In Yiddish."

Nicki managed to drink almost half a cup of coffee by swallowing it at the same time as the sweet bun. Then she helped Margo and Ira carry the dishes back inside.

"Everything was really good, Margo," she said. "How much do I owe you for this?" She pulled out her wallet.

"Your money's no good here, Yin," said Ira. He shoved a stack of plates into the dishwasher.

"He's right," added Ruthie. "And remember, you're welcome anytime."

"Thank you both, very much."

Margo walked Nicki outside.

"I like your parents," Nicki said.

"They're okay, I guess." Margo rolled her eyes. Then she smiled. "I love them."

"I know you do."

"So you're headed to the hospital?" asked Margo.

"I have to find out how Mr. Kahana's doing."

"You know anything I tell you is off the record, but—"

"Is he okay?"

Margo smiled. "Your feet must be tired. I might as well save you the trip to the hospital." She put a hand on Nicki's shoulder. "It sounds like Mr. Kahana is going to recover."

"Oh," sighed Nicki. "Thank goodness."

"I heard two nurses talking about how his vital signs were stronger and that the coma wasn't as deep as it had been. I think they expect him to come out of it."

"Thanks so much, Margo. That's such a relief, you've no idea." She took a deep breath.

"One thing, though," added Margo.

"What's that?"

"I don't want to upset you."

"You won't."

"The police have posted a second guard on the floor."

"A second guard?"

"Yes," said Margo. "I...I heard that—"

"What, Margo? What did you hear?"

"Someone tried to cut off Mr. Kahana's oxygen supply."

Chapter Eight

"Fenwick?"

"Miss Nicki? Where are you?"

"Still downtown. Is everything all right?"

"Splendid," said the butler. "And don't worry, the Ming is safe and sound."

"Good, because they think Grand Master Kahana may be out of the coma soon."

"Terrific news, Miss."

"I wish it were all good news, but..." She stopped. "Fenwick, did you do that reverse phone check for me?"

"The number is for Soong's Chinese Antiques," he replied, reading her the address on Spadina Avenue.

"A Chinese antique store?" She waited at a pedestrian crosswalk for the signal to change. "I wonder if he intended to sell the vase."

"Or maybe get an opinion as to its value."

"That could be it," agreed Nicki. "I'm going to check the place out."

"But aren't you coming home now? It's almost eight."

"Soong's must be just around the corner from here. I won't be long." She clicked off her phone and walked until she found the shop.

Dwarfed between two tall buildings, Soong's Chinese Antiques appeared uninhabited, except for a dim light burning at the back. In the window, a huge red-and-yellow sign read *One-of-a-Kind Finds*.

Bronze Buddhas and dragons with glassy eyes stared at her from the window, paintings of cherry blossoms and peonies on silk dangled from bamboo rods, ceramic panda bears, hardwood boxes, and incense burners sat in piles, and heaps of cheap-looking pottery took up any space that was left.

The curtain at the back of the store stirred when Nicki walked through the front door, and a bell jingled over her head. Before long, an elderly Chinese woman appeared.

"I'm psychic," she said.

"So am I," returned Nicki.

"Well, I suppose there's no point in conversation then. We'll just—"

"Read each other's minds? Okay." Nicki wandered around the store.

What a load of junk, she thought.

"This is not junk," the woman snapped. "These are unique, one-of-a-kind pieces. Why don't you treat yourself to a set of dishes? Or something to decorate your room?" She picked up a ceramic figurine.

"Okay, it's my turn," said Nicki. "You're wondering what I'm doing here. You figure I'm not going to buy anything—that I'm here with a hidden agenda."

"Maybe," said the woman.

Nicki took a business card from a stack on one of the tables.

"So you're Mrs. Soong?"

"My friends call me Lila."

"Okay, Lila, so why am I here?"

"I said *my friends* call me Lila." The woman put the figurine back in its place. "I know why you're here."

"Why?"

"To spy on my handsome grandson."

I'll bet he's not all that handsome.

"He is so," said Lila.

The woman can read minds! "I don't know your grandson." Nicki dragged her finger along the top of a picture frame. An inch of dust dropped to the floor. "I wouldn't get away with this where I work."

"Where *do* you work?"

"You're psychic. You tell me."

The woman didn't reply. Then she grinned.

"Okay," she said, "you can call me Lila."

"I work at a hotel, as a housekeeper."

Lila raised an eyebrow. "Give me a break," she said.

"I do," insisted Nicki.

Lila grabbed Nicki's hands and examined her palms. "These hands haven't ever done a day's hard work."

"I just started today," said Nicki, "so they have done one day's work."

"I'm thirsty. You?"

Nicki nodded.

Lila started for the back room, and Nicki followed.

"So is your handsome grandson's name Robert?"

Lila stopped dead in her tracks.

"No. My grandson is T'ai. Why do you ask if he is Robert?"

"I thought there might be someone here by the name of Robert. Robert A-G."

Lila rushed to the cash register, slid her hand under the counter, and pushed a button. Four times, maybe five.

"What are you doing?" asked Nicki.

Lila didn't reply.

A door banged shut.

Someone ran down from the apartment upstairs.

A young man of about eighteen pulled back the curtain.

He is good looking, thought Nicki, noticing his long, dark hair and muscular build.

"What's going on?" T'ai Soong looked at Nicki, then at his grandmother.

"She's asking about someone named Robert A-G."

T'ai grabbed Nicki by the arm. "Where's my uncle?"

"I don't know what you're talking about." She pulled herself free.

He grabbed her again, this time even harder.

Nicki figured she had two choices: employ a roundhouse kick to his ribs or feign weakness and find out who Robert A-G was and why David Kahana had his name.

She opted for the second choice.

Lila Soong's grandson dragged Nicki to the back room.

Chapter Nine

"Who are you?" asked T'ai.

"She's a spy," said Lila.

The bell over the front door jingled, and Lila peered through the curtains.

A young man with red hair walked in the front door. "It's your friend Mac," said Lila.

"We're back here," hollered T'ai.

"Why did you ask about Robert A-G?" Lila stared Nicki down.

"First, tell your grandson to let go of me," insisted Nicki.

T'ai and Lila exchanged glances.

Lila nodded.

"Robert," said T'ai, releasing Nicki, "is my great uncle. Lila's brother-in-law."

"My sister's husband," added Lila. "He's a widower now."

"So why did everyone freak out when I mentioned his name?" Nicki brushed off her arm. "And why did you ask if I'm a spy?"

"Robert's gone," said Lila.

"Gone?" asked Nicki.

"He was supposed to arrive here a week ago."

"And?" prompted Nicki.

"He never made it. Wasn't on the flight." Lila leaned against the wall and stared at her with black-marble eyes. "But you already knew that, right?"

"Of course not."

"Lila," said T'ai, "I believe her. I mean, look at her. She couldn't hurt a fly."

You might be surprised, Nicki said to herself.

"We've contacted everyone he knew in the States," added T'ai, "but he has vanished without a trace."

"He's from the States?" asked Nicki.

"He recently retired as a professor in the department of nuclear engineering at the Massachusetts Institute of Technology. He was coming to Toronto to meet someone, and to stay with us for a while."

"Now it's time to spill the beans." Lila moved three steps closer to Nicki. Then she turned to her grandson. "She knows something."

Nicki glanced through the curtains at the redhead. He was wandering around, picking things up, squeezing them, putting them back down again—as if he was in the produce section of a supermarket.

"Well?" prompted Lila.

"A friend of mine was sent to the hospital," explained Nicki, "and in his pocket was a slip of paper with Robert A-G and your phone number written on it. That's it. Really."

"What friend?"

"What does it matter?" Nicki shook her head in frustration.

Lila turned to T'ai. "I still say she's a spy. An agent for the People's Republic of China."

"I doubt it," said T'ai. "I believe her. You can see she's upset about her friend, Lila."

Nicki couldn't keep her eyes off the redhead. He strolled around aimlessly, finally wending his way to the cash register.

She couldn't be certain, because he was slightly out of her sight line, but Nicki was pretty sure he helped himself to some money.

"Come in here, Mac," said T'ai.

The young man's eyes were red and puffy and his complexion pale.

"Mac's a genius," said T'ai. "Like my uncle."

"So I'm a student at the University of Toronto in telecommunications engineering," Mac said. "Big deal."

"I'm a history major." T'ai pulled out a chair and sat down. The others followed suit. "To me, anyone who can do what Mac does is brilliant. What's that you're working on with your professor? Photonic crystals?"

"Photonic crystals?" asked Nicki.

"It's top secret," said T'ai. "It's going to change the whole smartphone industry. Explain it to her, Mac. I mean, the stuff you *can* talk about."

"Photonic technology uses light instead of electricity, so signals can be sent at extremely high speeds," he answered. "There's nothing secret about that."

"Yeah, but your professor's research is going to take the whole telecom industry by surprise," added T'ai. "And it will be used in medicine and aviation—right, Mac?"

Mac nodded.

Nicki noticed Mac's fingernails. They'd been chewed so far down, they were bleeding.

"So you've discovered a method of sending signals—differently? Faster?" she asked him.

"My professor has found a way to couple resonant cavities with emitters to controllably produce photons with telecommunications wavelengths."

Lila rolled her eyes.

"I don't know what he's talking about half the time," admitted T'ai, "but it's cutting-edge stuff."

Nobody said anything for a minute or two, then T'ai spoke up.

"My friend here does have a name—Duncan MacDonald," continued T'ai, pointing to his left. "You know Lila and I'm T'ai." He scratched his chin. "So who are you?"

"I'm Fu Yin."

"And this friend you mentioned?"

"David Kahana. He's American. From Honolulu." She

chose her words carefully. "I think he's the one who was supposed to meet your great uncle."

"What makes you think so?" asked T'ai.

"Because someone tried to kill him last night."

"What?" Lila's jaw dropped.

"He was stabbed."

"Oh, wow," muttered T'ai. "I'm sorry."

"He's going to recover." Nicki bit her bottom lip. "He has to."

"Is this Kahana person a CIA agent?" asked Lila.

"Or involved in intelligence?" added T'ai.

Nicki was about to answer when Mac got up to leave. Abruptly.

"I'm not feeling so good, T'ai. If you don't mind, I think I'll catch up with you tomorrow night instead."

"What's up with you, mate? Are you okay?"

"I'm tired, that's all." The two young men headed to the door. "T'ai," Nicki heard Mac whisper, "can you loan me a few bucks?"

"Again?" T'ai pulled out his wallet.

"I'll pay you back in a couple days. Please, man. I'm desperate."

T'ai handed him a twenty-dollar bill.

"That's forty bucks he owes," Lila shouted from the back room. "The twenty you just gave him, and another twenty for what he took out of the register."

Nicki listened as the clock on the wall beside her ticked away. A half hour had passed since Mac had left and she still hadn't gotten anywhere with the Soongs.

"Look," said Nicki, "I've told you what I know." She leaned back in the chair. "If you don't want to discuss it, I understand. But why are you two so fixated on espionage?"

"My great uncle worked for years at MIT. His research has led to great advances in nuclear technology."

"That's right," said Lila.

"My uncle's an honest man; a hardworking man. He believes that his work belongs to the country that has supported his research. Others find it more lucrative to sell technological secrets to foreign governments. Like Russia and China."

"I see," said Nicki.

"It was dangerous for him, but my uncle did what was right. He didn't stand for anything underhanded going on with his students or fellow researchers. And the CIA appreciated it. Both the CIA and the FBI knew of people out there who wanted him dead." T'ai fidgeted with his watchband. "And it looks like they may have succeeded."

"I think Mr. Kahana was here on behalf of the US government," said Nicki. "The Secret Service."

"I don't know anything about him. My uncle didn't tell us much, probably for our own safety."

"Obviously the wrong person found out that David Kahana was in Toronto, and now he's fighting for his life, and your uncle is—"

"Kidnapped," said T'ai.

Lila shuddered.

"Or dead," he said.

"Let's hope you're wrong. Have you contacted the police in Massachusetts?"

"Of course," said T'ai. "And the local police won't treat this as a missing-person case because they say my uncle left willingly and there was no sign of a struggle."

"Willingly…" Nicki thought about it. "So someone convinced him to go someplace other than Toronto."

"Right."

"And to travel under an assumed name."

"Probably."

"What about the FBI?"

T'ai let out a sarcastic laugh. "Yeah, right. Like they're going to let *me* in the loop."

Nicki picked up her jacket. "I've got to go," she said. "I work at the Haddon Heights hotel, so you can always find me there.

"By the way," she added, "what does A-G stand for?"

T'ai looked at Lila.

She shrugged her shoulders.

"Aisin-Gioro."

Nicki's bag dropped to the ground.

"You're kidding me."

Chapter Ten

"No," said T'ai, "I'm not kidding." He handed Nicki her bag. "He's a member of the Chinese royal family. What's left of it."

"But I thought Pu Yi, the boy emperor, had no children."

"He didn't. But he had plenty of nieces and nephews," T'ai explained.

"When the Manchu dynasty was overthrown in 1911, the family members were tossed out like garbage onto the streets," added Lila.

"Not quite, although it was a frightening time for the remnants of the Manchu imperial family," said T'ai. "My uncle has always wanted to return to his homeland and try to help some of his cousins, but—"

"He'd be thrown in prison as a traitor," said Lila.

Nicki nodded.

"Now I get it."

"What do you get?" asked Lila.

"I think I have something that might lead to your uncle."

★ ★ ★

"Here we are," said T'ai, holding the door for Nicki so she could carry her duffel bag with two hands.

The university cafeteria was packed with students and faculty members.

"You wouldn't think it would be so crowded this time of year," she said.

"Summer students trying to get in a few extra courses," said T'ai. "I'm taking one at night so I can help Lila during the day." He smiled. "We've got to convince the tourists that they need a trinket from Chinatown."

"I doubt your grandmother needs much help in that department."

"Right," said T'ai, directing her to a seat near the windows.

"Have you always stayed with your grandmother?" asked Nicki, wondering where T'ai's parents were and why he didn't live with them.

"I have for a few years," he said.

"What about your parents?"

"They're in Vancouver now. We don't get along too well."

"I'm sorry," Nicki said. *At least you know where they are,* she thought.

"What about you?" asked T'ai. "Are your parents—"

She cut him off immediately. "Are you sure this Dr. Byron knows where to meet us?"

"I called him last night after you left. We've met here before." T'ai removed his jacket, and Nicki placed her bag gently on the floor beside her feet. "He's a nice guy, for a professor. He's taken Mac and me out for lunch several times."

"And he's an expert in Chinese history?"

"He's a visiting professor. Sort of a research fellow, I guess, because he doesn't teach any courses. But that's his field all right."

"And you told him about the Ming?"

"I said a friend of mine had a vase and wanted to know its history. I said nothing about David Kahana."

Nicki looked around the cafeteria. "Good."

"Can I get you something?" asked T'ai.

"No, thanks." Nicki picked up a napkin and starting tearing little pieces from the edge.

"Nervous?"

"I guess."

"You don't have to work today?" he asked.

"No, tomorrow."

"On a Saturday? That's too bad." T'ai saw Byron from across the room. He stood up and waved to him. "Here he comes."

Nicki watched him weave his way through groups of people carrying trays of food and armloads of books.

"Dr. Peter Byron," said T'ai, "this is Fu Yin."

"Pleased to meet you," said Nicki, extending her hand.

"Thanks for agreeing to help us."

"I'm happy to do what I can," the professor replied.

"It's really very beautiful," said Nicki, pointing to her duffel bag.

"We can't look at it here," said Byron. "Too many students with nothing better to do than gape."

"How about your office?" asked Nicki.

"No, that's no good."

Why can't we go to his office? she wondered.

"Let me think," said Byron, placing an index finger on his chin. "There's got to be some quiet place nearby."

"Let's go to Mac's room," suggested T'ai. He turned to Nicki. "He lives here in residence."

"Good," said Byron, and the three of them headed across campus.

The door to Mac's room swung open when T'ai knocked. His friend was nowhere in sight.

"He must have a class. The guy never rests." T'ai closed the door behind the other two. "He won't mind if we come in."

Nicki removed several layers of bubble wrap from the vase.

Peter Byron was more interested in Mac's room and everything in it.

"Takes me back," he said. Then he opened a desk drawer. "Can I borrow a pen?" he asked. "I want to take some notes, then I can check my sources for information about your bowl."

"Vase."

Nicki watched his eyes skim back and forth across the desk drawer, as if he was searching for something. Finally, he picked up a pen. Then he looked for paper, but instead of going for blank sheets from an open package, he riffled through typed pages sitting in a pile next to Mac's printer.

"Here it is." Nicki handed the vase to Byron.

"Yes, that's a Ming all right," he said, then gave it to T'ai.

That's it? That's all you're going to say? "Can you tell me anything about it?" asked Nicki.

"What year would this have been fired?" T'ai gently turned the vase around. "Can you determine the age from the dragon design?" T'ai looked at the bottom. "I guess it would have been made in 1600 or so."

"Yes, yes," said Byron, "you're probably right."

Nicki watched his gaze shift back and forth between the vase and every book, file, and disk on Mac's desk.

What's this guy's problem?

"How do you know that the vase isn't from the Tang dynasty? Since that came immediately before the Ming period—wouldn't it be difficult to tell?"

T'ai went to correct her, but Nicki gestured him not to speak.

"Well, you can't be sure, of course. It could be a Tang vase." He scratched down something on the paper, tucked it into his shirt pocket, and went to put the pen back into the desk drawer, but dropped it.

"I'll get that," said T'ai, bending over to pick it up.

Byron's hand moved fast, but Nicki was sure he stuck something on the underside of the drawer.

Did he just plant a bug?

"I'll consult some of my colleagues and see what I can find out," he said. "But really, I think you'd better take this to an expert in ceramics. Maybe somebody at the Royal Ontario Museum."

"Yes," said Nicki, "the ROM has had exhibits of Chinese porcelain in the past. That's a good idea."

As she began to wrap the vase, Mac entered the room.

"What's going on?" His face turned bright red, and he stormed over to T'ai. "What! You think you can bust in here without even asking me?"

"But, the door was—"

"I don't care. Get out of here."

Nicki and Byron shuffled out to the hall.

"Mac, you always said I could—"T'ai stopped. "Your forehead. It's bruised." He moved closer. "What happened, Mac?"

"Forget about it."

He slammed the door in T'ai's face.

T'ai hollered through the crack.

"Mac, I'm sorry. Really. You said I could come here anytime."

There was no reply.

T'ai slapped his hand on the door several times, but Mac didn't open it. "Mac, are you coming to the dance tonight?"

Still nothing.

"Dance?" asked Nicki. "You mean that disco—retro—whatever dance?"

"Yeah, that's it." He leaned against the wall. "I haven't exactly been in the mood for fun lately, but it might get my mind off things for a while. Why don't you come?" He raised his voice. "I'll be back for you later, Mac."

Nicki looked at Byron. He was listening to every word they said. Then his cell phone rang.

"Gotta take this," he said. "Sorry I wasn't much help." He turned his back to them and moved aside to talk to his caller. He took a small pad out of one pocket and a pen out of the other.

Nicki watched him write something down and underline it.

He had a pen all along.

Chapter Eleven

"Okay, so you're right. There's no way that Byron is a professor of Chinese history," said T'ai. "But how did you know he'd get tripped up on dynasties like that?"

"Just a hunch," she said.

"A hunch? Come on."

"He seemed distracted."

"That's true," said T'ai.

"How long has Dr. Byron been taking you and Mac out for lunch?" Nicki asked.

"I don't know, a month maybe."

"You mentioned last night that Mac hasn't been himself lately. How long has that been going on?"

T'ai thought for a second.

"I get your point. But why?"

"I'm not sure." Nicki kept her duffel bag planted firmly on her lap during the subway ride. When it was time to exit near the ROM, she and T'ai waited for everyone else to push through the doors first and then made their way off the train.

A museum administrator gave them permission to speak with an expert in Chinese porcelain. They found Dr. Wong on the second floor putting together an exhibit of ceramic dishes from Northern China.

"Hello, sir," said T'ai. "We were wondering if you could spare a few minutes."

"Certainly." He removed the gloves he'd been using to handle the pieces and invited the two of them to sit down at his workbench.

Nicki placed her bag in front of Dr. Wong.

"So, what do we have here?"

"A Ming vase," said Nicki.

Dr. Wong looked over the top of his glasses at her.

"She's not kidding, sir." T'ai lifted out the vase and removed the wrap.

Dr. Wong said nothing. He turned the vase around several times, felt the thickness of the walls, and examined the bottom. He held it up to the light, then gently ran his finger along the rim.

"Excuse me a minute," he said, while he went to get a magnifying glass.

T'ai looked at Nicki and raised his eyebrows.

She shrugged her shoulders.

When the expert returned, T'ai had questions.

"How old is this vase? Do you think it was made at the imperial factory at Ching-te-Chen?"

"It is true that the finest pieces came out of the factories of that great porcelain town," agreed Dr. Wong, continuing his inspection with the magnifying glass. "Everything they needed was right there in the hills—the kaolin clay, the materials for glazes, the cobalt—everything."

Nicki spoke up. "I researched these markings on the bottom, and I think they are a signature. My book said this is the six-character mark of Wan Li."

Dr. Wong smiled and nodded.

Then she made a remark about the design on the vase, and Dr. Wong continued.

"Yes, the five-clawed dragon is wonderful, isn't it?"

"Is this a valuable vase?" asked T'ai. "I read on the Internet that one like it sold at auction for almost seven million dollars."

"I don't doubt it," said Dr. Wong. "You don't often see an underglaze of this color." He pointed to the deep red background. "Copper red was a very difficult shade to fire. The temperature had to be exactly right, or it would turn black. And in those days, they didn't have electric kilns, of course.

"A piece like this," he continued, "would have been created for the royal family—for the emperor."

Nicki and T'ai exchanged quick glances.

"And would this piece have been passed from the Ming emperor to the emperor of the Qing/Manchu dynasty?" she asked. "In other words, would it have been in the royal household during the time of Manchu rule?"

"Possibly. And if it were, it would be worth far more than seven million dollars. In fact," said Dr. Wong, "it would be priceless."

"What do you mean it *would* be priceless?" asked Nicki.

"This vase would be one of a kind," he said. Then he looked over the top of his glasses again. "If it were genuine." He sighed. "Unfortunately, this one is not. I'm sorry."

Nicki's heart sank.

"Are you sure?" asked T'ai.

"Positive," said Dr. Wong. "Oh, it's a very good replica—in fact, I'd say it's one of the best I've seen. Probably fired in 1920 or thereabouts, to serve as a duplicate of the one that belonged to the emperor."

"Are there many of these duplicates around?" asked Nicki.

"Just a minute," said Dr. Wong. He left the room and returned with a folio containing information about historic vases.

He leafed through quickly until he found what he was after.

"Yes, of course." he said. "This red underglaze with the five-clawed dragon design did belong to the Chinese imperial family. It was stolen from them before the overthrow of the Qing dynasty."

He pushed the folio across the table.

"Historians believe it may have ended up in Hawaii."

"Hawaii?" said T'ai.

Nicki nudged his leg.

"Yes," replied Dr. Wong. "Honolulu's Chinatown played

a crucial role in the birth of modern China. Sun Yat-sen, the revolutionary who put an end to the ruling monarchy, was born in Zhongshan but was educated in Hawaii."

"I've, uh…I've heard that there's a bronze statue of him in Honolulu," said Nicki.

"But not everyone wanted to see the end of the Manchu regime, and there is speculation that the vase was offered to anyone who could do away with Dr. Sun." Dr. Wong looked at the folio again. "You asked me about the number of duplicates that are in circulation." He thought for a minute. "This might be the only one. Whoever made it would have needed the original to copy from."

"How do you know this one is fake?" asked T'ai.

"When examining Chinese pottery and porcelain from this period," he continued, "you always begin with a question."

"What question?" asked Nicki.

"Where is the scratch on the Ming vase?" Dr. Wong smiled at his younger companions. "You see, the Chinese craftsmen were wonderful, the best in the world, and they took their work very seriously. And they knew that for a work of art to be truly beautiful, in the deepest sense, it had to contain a flaw. So, after the artist had created the most magnificent piece he could, he would add a tiny scratch, or a "wrong" spot of paint. Anything small just to make sure it was not perfect."

"Because perfection is not beautiful," said T'ai.

"Right," said Dr. Wong. "Perfection is lifeless," he added, as he left the room to replace the folio.

"Hawaii!" T'ai whispered to Nicki.

"I know, I know," she replied. "It looks like David Kahana brought the vase all right— the real one—to return to your uncle and his family. But where is it now?"

"And where is he?"

Chapter Twelve

"Oh, I'm sorry, Miss Nicki. I thought for sure it was a real Ming." Fenwick carried the vase to the mantle and placed it next to an antique clock. "It may be only a replica, but it's lovely nevertheless." Because Nicki was standing on her head, he bent over sideways to talk to her. "What would you like for dinner tonight?"

"Anything—anything at all. But I'll have to eat early. I'm meeting Margo Bloom at the deli before we go to the dance."

"How long do you have to stay like that?" asked the butler.

"Just a few more minutes," she replied. "A correct Wing Chun stance is like a piece of bamboo, firm but flexible, rooted but yielding. It's all about balance, Fenwick. A well-balanced body recovers faster from any type of attack."

"I see."

"You must be like a young tree that bends in the wind, then snaps back with force."

"Indeed." He nodded his head.

"Spaghetti."

"Pardon?"

"Spaghetti," said Nicki. "For dinner."

"Yin!" Margo called from the back of the deli. "Here I am!" She had a platter of smoked meat sandwiches in one hand and a plate of sour pickles in the other.

Ira and Ruthie were in the kitchen shoving dishes under a heat lamp and arguing about who it was that mixed up an order.

"Extra speck, Ira. Mrs. Eisenberg wanted extra speck."

"Mrs. Eisenberg doesn't need extra speck!"

"Be quiet, Ira," said Ruthie. "She'll hear you." Margo's mother pulled a tray of pickled fat out of the fridge.

"Business is better tonight," Nicki commented.

"Busy for a Friday," said Margo, rushing past with a coffee pot.

"You think this is busy," yelled Ira. "You should have seen this place twenty years ago. Now that was busy!"

Nicki followed Margo out of the kitchen.

"Sit down anyplace," Margo said. "I'll be ready in a minute or two." She served a table of six, carried several loads of dishes to the back, wiped and reset a booth, and put on another pot of coffee.

"Okay, Yin," she said. "Let's go upstairs."

The two girls headed up to Margo's room. It was clean and bright and had a mural of a garden painted on the wall.

"Pretty good, eh?"

"Did you do that?"

"Sure did. I love flowers." She smiled. "I'm so glad you decided to come tonight." She looked at Nicki. "But you can't wear that."

"I'm just coming to watch. I won't be dancing."

"Sure you will. And here's what you'll be wearing."

She pulled a red dress out of her closet. It still had the price tag dangling from it.

"That's your new dress, Margo!"

"It'll look better on you."

"No, I don't want—"

"I won't take no for an answer. Put it on."

"It won't fit. I'm too short." Nicki slipped into the dress. "See?"

"Come on," said Margo, grabbing Nicki by the arm.

"Where?"

"Just come," she insisted, and she dragged Nicki back down into the deli.

"Mom!" hollered Margo, "can you hem this up for us?" Margo turned to Nicki. "My mother is a whiz with a needle and thread."

"But this is *your* dress, Margo. I can't take it." *I don't want it!* said Nicki to herself.

"I've got lots of dresses," chirped Margo.

"Too many dresses," echoed Ira.

Mrs. Bloom shoved Nicki onto a stool in the middle of the kitchen, and the two of them had the dress shortened and taken in at the waist in less time than it took Ira to grate a chunk of cabbage.

"Oh, that's great." Margo went up to her room, threw on a blue dress, and ran back down.

Nicki felt like a fool.

"What size shoe do you wear?" asked Margo.

Nicki drew the line. "No, I don't wear heels. Really, I can't."

Before Nicki knew it, Ira had cleared out the entire middle section of the deli. He'd pushed four or five tables to one side, connected his CD player to the speakers, and had disco music playing so loud that people walking outside stopped to listen.

And watch.

"Okay, everybody, get ready for something special. For those of you who don't know her already, this is my daughter Margo. Isn't she beautiful? Did I tell you that my beautiful daughter is going to be a nurse?"

"Yes, Ira," said a woman by the window. "About a hundred times."

"Did I tell you that my beautiful daughter has been named volunteer of the month at the hospital?"

"Yes, Ira."

Nicki looked at Margo.

Margo nodded, and Nicki gave her a thumbs up.

"Okay, sweetheart, are you ready?" called Ira.

Nicki looked puzzled, and Margo explained.

"My dad used to be a disco dance champion back in Brooklyn."

"She was the only girl at our synagogue to have a disco-themed bat mitzvah." Ruthie laughed as Ira and Margo bounded to the middle of the dining room and waited for the next song to start—"Jive Talkin'" by the Bee Gees.

It's just your jive talkin'
You're tellin' me lies, yeah,
Jive talkin'
You wear a disguise...

Nicki watched in amazement as Margo and her dad did every move in the book, from underarm turns to shadow steps. Every few bars, they separated and did solo steps; Ira threw an arm up straight, pulled back his shoulders, and moved his feet like a dancer right out of a movie.

All that jive,
You'll never know...

"Come on, Ira," yelled a customer, "let's see the Night Fever Line hustle!"

Nicki turned to Ruthie.

"They're really good," she said.

"Yeah, they are."

"Your husband is certainly proud of Margo."

Ruthie smiled. "Ira loves our daughter. He's loved her from the minute he laid eyes on her. We both have."

She's a lucky girl, thought Nicki. And then, out of nowhere, she felt tears forming in the corner of her eyes.

She wiped them away quickly, but Mrs. Bloom noticed.

"I'm sure your parents love you just as much, Yin," she said.

Which parents? Nicki asked herself. *The people who have given me everything I could possibly want, or the parents who probably had nothing to give? The Haddons, who look after my every need, but who can't find the time to watch me compete and who never ask about my dreams? Or the man and woman in China who might be dreaming dreams for me? Praying I'm alive. Hoping I'm happy.*

A surge of emotion flowed like lava from a volcano into Nicki's chest, into her heart.

The tears started to stream.

Don't be such a baby, she told herself. *Get a grip!*

But there was no way for her to contain it. She ran to the washroom.

Chapter Thirteen

Nicki bit into her knuckles to stop herself from crying. Then she sprayed cold water onto her face and dried it off with a wad of paper towels.

The door opened.

"You okay?"

"Fine, Margo." She pushed back her bangs. "Listen, I've been rethinking this whole dance thing. It's really not me."

"Oh, come on—"

"I don't feel up to it."

"Please," said Margo. "If you don't like it, we can leave after ten minutes. I promise."

Nicki looked at herself in the mirror. *What's wrong with you tonight?*

She spoke to Margo's reflection. "You're a good dancer.

Your dad is too," she said. "That must have been some bat mitzvah."

"It was, Yin. I'll never forget it." Margo adjusted the thin straps of her metallic blue dress. It was cut above the knee and had a tulip hem. Nicki's dress was made from a stretch satin and her black hair was positively striking against the bright red fabric. For a moment she wondered what T'ai would think of it.

"Now come on, let's go," urged Margo. "You said you had some friends who wanted to meet up with you at the dance."

"That's true."

"Then you'll come?"

It would give me a chance to get to know Duncan MacDonald better. See what he's up to.

"Only if you'll let me pay for this dress," insisted Nicki.

Margo thought about it.

"I'd be much happier if you'd accept it as a gift," she said. "You've just started working, and I'm sure money is tight. But I've got an idea. Come here and I'll show you something."

They went back into the deli and on a shelf behind the cash register was a big empty pickle jar with some change in the bottom of it. On the side was a picture of a palm tree cut out of a magazine, stuck down with a piece of masking tape on which the words *Honeymoon Jar* had been printed in black ink.

"After you've been working for a while, and have whatever you need for yourself, I'll let you put a couple of dollars into my parents' honeymoon jar, okay?" She held up her index finger. "No more than that."

"They haven't had a honeymoon yet?"

"They couldn't afford one when they got married, then they were busy trying to get the business going, then I came along. You know how it goes." She picked up the pickle jar. "So whenever we get an extra tip or something, we put it in here." She shook the money around. "They almost had enough once, but the refrigerator and oven broke within a week of each other."

Ira walked by with a huge container of coleslaw.

"We'd hoped by our tenth anniversary we could go. Then it was our fifteenth. Our twenty-fifth is next month, but it looks like it'll take until our thirtieth."

"Oh, come on Ira," said Ruthie. "Get real. If we make it to Hawaii by our *fiftieth*, we'll be doing something."

"Hawaii?" asked Nicki.

"That's their dream." Margo took a customer's credit card and rang through his bill. "Thanks a lot," she said, handing the man a receipt. She turned to Nicki and lowered her voice. "I really hope they can go for their silver anniversary. I've been thinking about putting off nursing school for a year and giving them what I've saved up—"

"You know what you can do with that idea?" Ira shouted from the kitchen. "Forget about it!"

★　★　★

"I hope you don't mind stopping off here for a minute first," said Nicki.

"This is a social visit," Margo warned the nurses at the desk.

"Don't get any big ideas about putting me to work tonight."

"I didn't even recognize you without the stripes," joked an older nurse.

"Nurse Cherry Ames, out on the town," said another.

"I love Cherry Ames." Margo swung her purse over her shoulder playfully.

"Who's she?" asked Nicki.

"Oh, you know—Cherry Ames, from the series of books for girls. She's like Nancy Drew, only a nurse. My grandmother gave me her set."

"Right. They were in your bookcase."

"I cherish them. Those books changed my life."

Nicki started for Kahana's room.

Margo clicked behind, her heels hitting the floor like it was a steel drum.

Nicki turned down the west corridor and immediately noticed the hall was completely empty. There was no guard at David Kahana's door.

Where's the guard?

Nicki picked up her pace. She grabbed the door handle and tugged until it opened.

Kahana was gone!

"Margo, he's not here!" gasped Nicki.

"He was fine when I left here today," said Margo. "Maybe they've just taken him—"

Nicki didn't wait for her to finish the sentence. She wheeled around and ran back to the nurses' station. Margo hurried behind.

From around the corner came Newman.

What's he doing here? Nicki's mind was racing. "Where's Master Kahana?"

"I was just about to ask that myself," said Newman.

"They've taken him upstairs for tests," replied a nurse. "But it's past visiting hours. You'll all have to leave."

Nicki let out a huge sigh of relief. "Are his guards with him?"

"Yes, of course," declared the nurse.

Nicki thanked her and then confronted the hotel manager.

"Mr. Newman," asked Nicki, "are you a friend of Mr. Kahana's?"

"Mr. Kahana was a guest at my hotel."

Your hotel? thought Nicki.

Newman directed his gaze squarely at Nicki. "Now I have a question for you. What are *you* doing here?" he asked. Before Nicki could answer, Margo jumped in.

"She's going to be taking lessons from him. When he's better. She's learning self-defense."

I wish she hadn't said that, thought Nicki.

"Okay," said the nurse, "everyone must leave now."

They all strolled toward the elevator. Newman got on, but Nicki stopped Margo before she could enter.

"Wait, Margo," she said, "I left my wallet in your locker!"

"Locker?"

The door shut on Newman.

"What are you talking about?" asked Margo.

"I want to speak to the nurse again."

The girls headed back to the reception area.

"Excuse me," said Nicki, "but that man who just left—Mr. Newman—does he come by here often? To ask about Mr. Kahana?"

"I'm sorry," said the nurse. "I can't give out that kind of information." She returned to her desk.

"She can't, but I will," whispered Margo as they walked away. "I've seen him here quite a few times. And yes, he's always inquiring about Mr. Kahana's condition."

"I thought so," said Nicki.

Chapter Fourteen

"Margo," said Nicki, raising her voice so she could be heard over the music, "this is T'ai Soong and his friend, Duncan MacDonald."

"Mac," replied the engineering student. He smiled at Margo and, wasting no time, asked her to dance.

T'ai showed Nicki to their table. "You look nice," he said.

"I feel ridiculous," she replied. "Anyway, Mac seems to be in a better mood tonight."

"Yeah, I guess. Still not the guy I grew up with though. Believe it or not, he used to be a lot of fun."

"He's changed."

"Oh, for sure. Like today—he got rid of his cell phone. And when I asked him why, he said they're too easily tapped into." T'ai rolled his eyes. "He told me that with the right equipment, it's possible to remotely activate the microphone, even when a call is not being made, to listen to nearby conversations."

"I guess he'd know."

"Right, but when I joked with him and asked him what he had to hide, he got furious." T'ai shrugged. "It's as if he's lost his sense of humor."

Mac and Margo appeared behind T'ai.

"Who's lost their sense of humor?"

"You."

"You're a jerk." Mac took Margo by the arm, then turned to Nicki. "Your friend is a terrific dancer," he said, leading her back to the floor.

"See what I mean?" said T'ai. Then he looked at Nicki. "I'm sorry. Did you want to dance?"

"Not really. It's not my thing," she replied. "You don't have to sit here with me, though. I'm happy to watch."

"I don't feel like dancing either."

"Thinking about your uncle?"

"He goes through my mind all the time. I put in another call to the Massachusetts state police today, but they can't tell me anything. Or won't." T'ai stood up. "I think I'll get a soda. What can I get you?"

"Sparkling water would be great, thanks."

Nicki looked around while T'ai was gone. Circling the club, she scanned everyone on the dance floor and at the tables.

She watched as Mac and Margo moved across the floor. Dancing and talking, they were oblivious to the fact that they were being watched. And not only by Nicki.

Just outside the washrooms, two young men in black leather never took their eyes off Mac. And across from them, in an alcove near the fire exit, stood an older man, watching everything from behind dark sunglasses. He didn't remove them until Mac and Margo left the floor.

Peter Byron!

Nicki returned to the table.

"Where were you?" asked Margo. "And why aren't you dancing?" She waved to some friends of hers across the aisle.

T'ai came back, carrying the drinks. He passed Nicki her water.

"Aren't you going to ask Yin to dance?" Margo gave T'ai a nudge.

"I did." He sat down. "Anyway, who wants to compete with you two?"

"Where did Mac go?" Nicki asked.

"I don't know," said Margo. "He was here a minute ago." She twisted around and saw him talking with the disc jockey.

"Just a second," she said, and headed there herself.

"T'ai," said Nicki, "I saw Byron."

"Really?"

"I'm sure it was him."

"Why would he be hanging out here, I wonder."

"I don't know, but"—she looked up and over T'ai's head—"here he comes."

"May I join you?"

"Sure." T'ai pushed out a chair with his foot.

"Mac here?" asked Byron.

"Yes," said Nicki. *But you already knew that.*

"He's requesting a song," said T'ai, pointing to Mac and Margo. "Here he comes now."

"You guys are no fun," said Margo. "Who can resist this one?" she asked, while "I Will Survive" blasted across the club.

"Your selection, Mac?" asked T'ai caustically. Mac ignored him and swung past the table with Margo in tow.

Nicki followed Byron's gaze to the washroom, and to the two guys in black leather. One of them, who appeared to be Chinese, pulled a cell phone out of his pocket and handed it to the other, a blond, who left the room to make a call.

"Friends of yours?" asked Nicki.

Byron didn't reply.

The blond returned, signaled the other guy, and the two bounced onto the dance floor and headed straight for Mac.

Byron jumped up.

"What's going on?" asked T'ai.

The two guys grabbed Mac and dragged him to the fire exit door. Margo stood in horror as one of them pulled out a knife and forced Mac outside.

Nicki ran after them.

They threw Mac against the wall.

"Come on, Quon," said Mac. "Give me another couple of days."

"Your time's up, pal," said Quon. "Pay me now, or you're history. Understand?" He punched Mac in the face. "Your turn, Phil," he said with a smirk.

Phil held the knife under Mac's neck, then kneed him hard in the stomach. Mac fell to the ground. Quon picked him up and punched him again. "You're all out of options, MacDonald. Give me the money or we'll use the blade."

"Don't even think about it." Nicki deftly kicked the knife out of Phil's hand, then shoved it with her foot so it slid underneath a parked van. "Let him go."

Quon laughed. "Why should I?"

Before Nicki could reply, the fire exit door flew open and two bouncers muscled out. T'ai and Margo were with them. They tried to get Mac to his feet, but he was coughing blood.

Quon had the last word.

"We'll be seeing you, MacDonald. You can count on it."

Nicki trailed them for several blocks, across intersections, down a side street, and through a park. They turned down a narrow alley that ran behind a row of older buildings, then into the back entrance of a run-down, two-story apartment house.

Nicki made her way down the alley. She wanted to follow them inside, but looked down at her dress.

Oh, I can't do anything in this, she thought.

By the time she'd made it back to the club, T'ai and Margo had ice on Mac's eye. The three of them were sitting on the ground with their backs against the brick building.

"Yin!" cried Margo.

"I know where they live," said Nicki.

"Who cares?" She threw her arms around Nicki.

"Thanks for what you did," mumbled Mac.

"He won't let me take him to the hospital," said Margo. "I'm worried about internal bleeding."

"Look, I can't go," said Mac. "They'll call the police, and if they do, I'm a dead man."

"What do these guys have on you?" asked T'ai.

Mac wouldn't answer.

"Come on, Mac. I'm your best friend," T'ai pleaded. "Why are they after you?"

Mac stared at the ground.

"Okay, that's it," declared T'ai. "I've had it with you. And this time, I mean it." He got up and left.

"You know," said Mac, watching his best friend walk away, "I wish they *had* killed me." He coughed several times. "Life isn't worth living anymore."

Chapter Fifteen

"I don't know how Ellen managed to get today off," said Dolores, as she and Nicki filled their cleaning cart with supplies. "I hate working on Saturday, don't you?"

"Yes," said Nicki. "Especially when it's so nice outside."

"Too hot for me."

"I don't mind the heat," said Nicki. "I like to run first thing in the morning, though, before the worst of it sets in."

"You're ambitious. I drag myself out of bed, drink two or three cups of coffee, and convince myself that I'm going to win the lottery." She laughed. "Ready to go?"

"Ready as I'll ever be."

They pulled the cart into the service elevator, got off on the fourth floor, and knocked at 401.

"Housekeeping. Anybody there?" When nobody answered,

Dolores put her key card in the slot. "I knew he wouldn't be here, but I always follow the rules."

"You knew who wouldn't be here?"

"The manager."

"This is Trent Newman's room?" asked Nicki.

"Yep," replied Dolores. "Which is why I always follow the rules." She knocked again, then opened the door and went inside. Nicki took a wet rag and started to clean the safe. While wiping it off with one hand, she tried to open it with the other.

It was locked.

She waited for Dolores to go into the washroom, then used the override key.

The safe was empty.

"How long has Newman lived here?" asked Nicki when Dolores returned.

"Not long at all," she replied. "He moved out of his apartment recently. He's staying here until he finds a new place, I guess."

"Ever find anything interesting in here?" Nicki pulled the sheets off the bed and threw them onto a cart in the hall.

"Nothing more interesting than wine bottles." She helped Nicki stretch the fitted sheet onto the mattress. "And Spam."

"Yeah," said Nicki, "he does love his Spam."

Dolores fluffed the pillows and put on new cases.

"There was one weird thing," said Dolores.

"What?"

"A Mandarin dictionary." She shrugged her shoulders. "What would he want with a Chinese dictionary?"

★ ★ ★

When Nicki finished her shift at five-thirty that afternoon, she found T'ai waiting by the main desk.

"I figured you'd be around here somewhere," he said. "I wanted to apologize for taking off last night. I wasn't mad at you."

"I know," replied Nicki. "And I don't blame you for being frustrated with Mac." She looked around the lobby. "Since you're here, do you want to help me with something?"

"Sure. What's up?"

"I want to search the manager's office."

"You think this guy's involved?"

"I don't know." She pulled out her mother's override key and opened the door to Newman's office.

"Where did you get that?" asked T'ai.

"Who cares? Point is, I have it."

T'ai shut the door quietly behind them.

"We'll have to work fast," Nicki said.

She switched on the desktop computer. "I don't see his laptop around here, do you?"

"No, just the hotel computer," answered T'ai. "How did you get the access password to this thing anyway?"

"I work here, remember?"

T'ai sat down and started opening files.

"What, exactly, am I hacking into here?"

Nicki started searching through CDs in a case behind his desk. "I need to find the surveillance footage of the eighth-floor hallway on the night David Kahana was knifed— Wednesday night, around eight-thirty or so. I need to know who entered his room from that time on."

T'ai clicked away, and Nicki watched over his shoulder. "I know Newman's connected. I just don't know how."

They shoved discs in and out of the computer until they came to surveillance footage of Wednesday night.

"Look at that," said Nicki. "It's been erased."

"How can you tell?" asked T'ai.

"The time stamp doesn't match up. Look here." She replayed the tape. "Nothing but an empty hallway, except for the odd person with a suitcase coming on or off the elevator. But notice how the counter stops at ten thirteen, then starts again fifteen minutes later. Enough time for Newman to go upstairs, walk through the hall, enter the room, and return to his office."

"For sure," said T'ai.

"Nobody else but Newman has access to these tapes."

Nicki thought for a minute. "What about the record of room 813? Was it opened on Wednesday night around that time?"

T'ai found the files for the rooms.

"Yes." He pointed to the screen. "The universal key opened Mr. Kahana's door at ten nineteen."

"So Newman erased the videotape of himself, but not the record of the entry." Nicki looked at T'ai. "Maybe there's no way to erase that."

T'ai shrugged his shoulders.

"I don't know. Mac could tell you." He leaned back. "But I don't want his help."

Nicki didn't comment.

"So," continued T'ai, "Newman had time to stick the fake vase in the safe. But so what?" He got up. "We can't prove anything."

"Not yet," said Nicki.

She sat down at the computer and started searching for downloaded files that might help.

"Just hotel records, documents, payments. Nothing interesting," she mumbled.

Then she found something.

"Look at this," she said. "In his e-mail program—his list of contacts." She ran her finger down the screen and pointed to a name.

"Peter Byron?" T'ai shrugged. "They know each other?"

Nicki heard something moving outside the door and gestured to T'ai.

"What do we do now?" he whispered. He opened the door a tiny bit. "There's a man out there. I don't know who he is. He's talking to the concierge."

Nicki looked out.

"That's Newman!" she said. She snapped off the computer.

"Now what?" asked T'ai.

Nicki spotted a first aid kit and yanked it off the wall.

"Get down on the floor," she said, "and follow my lead."

The door opened.

Newman looked at Nicki. Then at T'ai. Then at Nicki again.

"Nobody—and I mean nobody—enters this office when I am not here! This is the end of the line for you. I'm not kidding."

"I can't talk now," she said, slapping the sides of T'ai's face. "Quick," she told Newman. "Look in there. Do you have something to revive him?" She pushed the first aid kit toward him. Everything spilled out onto the floor, including a half-used bottle of iodine.

"What happened to him?" Newman tried to stop the iodine from flowing out of the bottle.

"I don't know," she said. "He just collapsed. His pulse is weak. Help me, please."

"Did you call 911?" he asked.

Nicki couldn't think up an answer fast enough. She pinched T'ai, and he opened his eyes and coughed.

"Wha…what happened?"

"You were feeling ill, sir. I brought you into Mr. Newman's office to get first aid, but you passed out. Can you stand up now?"

T'ai slowly got to his feet.

"Are you…all right?" Newman asked.

"I think it's the heat. I…I just need some water."

Nicki supported T'ai, and the two staggered out of the office.

Newman slammed the door shut.

T'ai rubbed his cheeks.

"Did you have to be so convincing?"

Chapter Sixteen

"Fenwick? Where are you, Fenwick?" Nicki called from outside the subway station on her way to the university residence. After several attempts, she left a message.

"Fenwick, I won't be back in time for dinner tonight. It's already past six, and I'm on my way downtown." She went to click off the phone, then spoke again. "Where are you, anyway? I've called a dozen times."

"I'm here, Miss." The butler was out of breath. "I've just returned home from the market. I found some lovely *champignons*." She could hear bags rustling in the background.

"How about tomorrow night?" asked Nicki.

"Splendid," said Fenwick.

Nicki walked across campus to the building that housed Mac's room. Two girls her age stopped her to ask directions to the English department, where orientation for the upcoming fall semester was about to take place.

"I'm sorry, I couldn't tell you," admitted Nicki.

"That's okay, we'll find it." The first girl opened up a folder to check a map of the campus.

"So what are you going to be studying?" the second girl asked Nicki.

"I'm, uh…I won't be taking classes," she said. "Not here."

"York?" the girl asked Nicki, referring to another university in Toronto.

"No, I'm not planning on university."

"Oh, that's too bad," said the other girl, with a hint of insincerity in her voice that Nicki detested. "It's going to be great."

I don't have time for it, Nicki told herself. *Not now. I want to focus on my training.*

The two girls chatted and pointed and went on their way, so excited about their future at the university, their feet hardly hit the ground.

That's not for me.

Mac's door was open, and he was working at his computer. A large bandage taped neatly under his eye and an even larger bottle of pain medicine next to his bed could only mean one thing.

"Margo been to see you?" asked Nicki from the hallway.

She wasn't going to make the mistake of entering Mac's room until invited to do so.

"Hi. Come on in." Mac swiveled his chair around to face her. "She was here earlier today. Quite the nurse, isn't she?"

Nicki nodded.

"Sit down," said Mac, pointing to the end of the bed.

He flipped his computer screen off, but not before Nicki got a glimpse of the web page he'd been on. It was a gaming site.

And he wasn't winning.

"I came to see how you were doing, Mac," said Nicki.

"And to ask a few questions?"

"Maybe."

"I wish I could answer them, but I can't. You're a nice person, and so is Margo. I don't want to drag you into this. It's my problem."

"By not telling T'ai what's going on with you, Mac, you're going to lose a friend."

He picked up a pencil and broke it in half.

"Do you think I don't know it?" He hurled the pieces against the wall. And then, under his breath, he mumbled something that said it all. "I'll get out of this mess one day. Things are going to change."

"You won't solve your problems by gambling. All you're going to do is make somebody else rich."

Mac said nothing.

"It's none of my business, though," added Nicki.

"Right."

Mac turned his chair back to face the computer, which Nicki read as her sign to leave.

"I have to get some work done," he snapped. When Nicki got up to leave, he grabbed her sleeve. "I'm sorry."

"For what?"

"I don't know." He rubbed his eye with the back of his hand. "For everything."

"I'll see you around."

Nicki stood in the hallway for a minute. She could hear him roll back to the computer and start tapping his money away again.

Then he stopped abruptly.

"No!" he screamed.

Nicki figured he must have maxed out his credit card. Nothing else would make him quit.

He took his anger out on the desk, bashing it with his fist.

He kicked the door shut.

Nicki took the stairs down and sat for a minute on a bench near the front entrance to tie her shoelace. When she looked up, she saw Mac heading across the grass.

He must have used the back stairway. She jumped up to see where he was going. Under his arm he carried a manila envelope, folded over and taped down. *He's in an awful rush,* she thought.

She followed him to the subway platform and watched as he stood there, hesitating, trying to decide whether to board the train or not. Twice he held back as everyone pushed through the door. Finally, he boarded the third train to pull into the station.

Nicki followed suit.

She buried herself in the crowd, observing Mac as they rumbled along. The expression on his face was one of worry, fear—and dread. He got off two stops later.

Nicki followed.

He looked at his watch and then picked up his pace.

He crossed an intersection before the signal had changed and dashed through a park—the same park through which Nicki had followed his attackers the night before.

Down a side street he rushed, until he came to the narrow alley.

He's heading straight to Quon!

Nicki kept on his heels, waited for him to enter through the back door of the apartment house, then she headed down the alley.

The door was broken, and through the jagged glass, she could hear Quon's threats.

"So you finally came to your senses," he said, his voice cold, his words blunt. "If you expect to leave here with both arms attached, MacDonald, those better be the discs."

Chapter Seventeen

Quon led Mac up a flight of stairs.

Nicki looked up and saw a window being propped open by a piece of wood. She scrambled down the alley and found an old crate to stand on. She dragged it to the window and jumped up on it. She wasn't quite high enough to see inside, so she grasped the cement window ledge and pulled herself up, with nothing but her arm muscles to hold her in place.

She was peering into someone's kitchen, but it wasn't Quon's.

A woman and her son sat with their elbows resting on a table. Surrounded by the supper dishes and deeply engrossed in a board game, they didn't see Nicki's face at their window.

She lowered herself down.

Okay. His place must be on the second floor.

Nicki looked up again. There were two windows, both open, and one of them had a platform beneath it with a steel railing around it. Too small to be a balcony, but big enough to stand on and hopefully get inside the room.

But she had to climb up there first.

Running down the side of the building, not far from the window with the platform, was a metal downspout that led to the eaves trough along the roof. It was secured into the brick with bolts.

Pushing her feet into the wall and propelling herself upward along the spout, she managed to make it to the second-floor level.

Then came the difficult part—jumping to the platform without falling two stories down to the alley.

She swung her feet and got a toehold on the outside edge of the tiny balcony, then pivoted so she could grab the metal rail with one hand. Once she had hold of it, she managed to spring across and climb over the top.

She pushed back a pair of filthy curtains, leaned through the window, and checked out the bedroom.

The bed was unmade, clothes were strewn everywhere, and beer bottles were left on every conceivable surface at various stages of consumption.

She clambered in and crept through the room and into the hallway.

From her vantage point, she could see into the kitchen.

A young man and woman sat at a table with Quon and Mac; she recognized the man as Phil from the dance, and Nicki heard Quon call the woman Rita. Two gold rings pierced her left eyebrow, and a tattoo of a noose graced her upper arm.

"Okay, MacDonald," said Quon, "you'd better not be yanking my chain this time."

Quon ripped open the manila envelope, shook out several computer discs, then went to the fridge and pulled out a beer. He twisted the cap off with his teeth, took two swigs, then stuck one of the discs into his laptop.

"Where's the hard copy?"

"Everything I have is on disc."

Nicki positioned herself perfectly, turned on her cell phone camera, and aimed it for the table.

Quon put in another disc.

"This is it?"

"Those files represent the findings of the best minds in the world. My professor and his team have been working on this for eighteen months."

"What's it about?" Quon rubbed his lips.

"We've found a way to create a 3-D photonic crystal that is both electronically and optically active."

"I don't know," mumbled Quon.

"What don't you know?" Mac's voice resounded with both anger and fear.

"It'll have to be cleared with the boss."

"Who is your boss anyway?" asked Mac.

Quon laughed.

"Yeah, right."

"Is he in Beijing?"

"Let's just say he travels quite a bit." His voice trailed off as he got up to open a bag of potato chips. He took a knife out of his pocket, slashed the bag, then slit it down the middle. "How about a round with my friends here. Double or nothing. If you're lucky, you'll win and be able to clear the rest of your debt."

"I've cleared my debt. I've just handed China enough intellectual property to satisfy a thousand debts." Nicki heard him bang his fist on the table. "They'll jail me for the rest of my life for this."

Quon laughed again.

"How about a little game of five card draw, Mac?"

Nicki could hear Mac get up and push out his chair.

Phil grabbed him and thrust him back down. "You don't go anyplace until Quon says you do."

Quon took another gulp of beer. "I'll loan you the cash to play. Maybe tonight is your lucky night. Everyone has a good night now and then, right?"

"Maybe," said Mac.

No! thought Nicki. *Don't give in!*

"Okay then, everyone," said Phil, "let's deal."

Nicki heard the slap, slap, slap of the cards. She bent her wrist as far back as she could to allow her camera to get a full shot of Quon and his guests. When she did, her foot hit the baseboard.

"What was that?"

Quon jumped up.

Nicki quickly rolled herself against the wall.

"I heard something," he repeated.

"Me too." Rita got out of her chair and looked around.

Nicki's heart started to pound. She felt beads of sweat forming on her forehead and rolling down her cheeks.

"Forget it, Quon," said Phil. "Let's play."

Slap, slap, slap.

Nicki sighed in relief as she positioned her phone back in place.

"Okay, Rita, here comes the jack. You deal, baby."

"Cut," said Phil.

"Done."

They dealt until they each had five cards.

"Okay." Phil pushed his chips to the center of the table.

"I'll straddle," said Quon, moving even more chips in.

"Pass," said Rita.

Mac turned to Quon.

"I'll see you and double the ante." He shoved in a mound of chips.

Oh, Mac, thought Nicki.

"I'll see you and raise—" Nicki couldn't make out his exact words, but by the number of chips he sent to the middle of the table, it was clear the blackmailer's bet was huge.

"You're bluffing," said Mac.

Quon took a swig of beer and belched in his face.

Phil threw down his hand and passed.

Mac raised the stakes again.

Showdown time.

"Full house," said Mac, laying out three tens and two threes.

Quon smiled.

Then he fanned his cards in front of Mac.

"Sorry pal," he mocked, spreading out a straight flush—ace, king, queen, jack, and ten of hearts.

He stood up.

"I guess that's another grand you owe me, MacDonald. Unless you care to go double or nothing?"

No! Don't do it!

Slap, slap, slap went the cards for another hour. Nicki's cell phone memory had maxed out, but it didn't matter. She had enough evidence to send Quon away until his crew cut turned gray. Maybe longer.

The only problem was that T'ai's best friend would be going with him.

They played until Mac could stand the defeat no more. Now owing more than six thousand dollars, he hurled the cards across the room.

"I'll be in touch, Mr. MacDonald," declared Quon, "to make arrangements."

"I've given you everything. There's nothing left to take."

"Oh, come on," said Quon. "You must know a few more professors in the engineering department. My boss would love to know what kinds of things they've come up with for smartphones. And you're the man to give it to him."

"I can't do that."

"Figure something out."

As he got up to leave, Nicki could hear Mac moaning something to himself.

"I'll kill myself first."

And by the expression on his face, the look of a completely destroyed individual, Nicki knew he wasn't kidding.

Mac was about to commit suicide.

Chapter Eighteen

Nicki watched as Quon and Phil followed Mac downstairs and Rita went into the washroom. She knew she had about thirty seconds to get the discs and get out of the apartment.

She ran into the kitchen. They weren't on the table.

Quon didn't take them with him—they had to be there someplace. Frantically, she scoured the room.

At last she spotted the envelope on the far counter, on the opposite side of the room.

Quon was on his way back up the stairs.

And she heard a toilet flush.

She took a chance.

She darted across the room and grabbed the envelope, but it was too late.

Rita spotted her.

"Quon!" she hollered.

Quon's eyes turned black with rage. "You're that chick from the dance. How the…how did you get in here?" He grabbed his knife.

Nicki dashed to the bedroom and fired the discs out the window. They flew out of the envelope and, like Frisbees, shot in every direction. The alley had no illumination whatsoever. Everything, other than a dull yellow light coming from the apartment below, was pitch black.

She threw her leg over the windowsill.

Quon grabbed the sleeve of her shirt and started pulling her back in. He hollered down the alley to Phil. And as he wrapped his arm around Nicki's shoulders, he held his knife to her throat.

Savagely, he ripped the gold chain from her neck, and her good-luck charm fell to the floor.

"Give me that!" she screamed.

He laughed, snapped it up off the ground, and starting examining it. "It's a piece of junk."

"Get your hands off it."

With a pressure point thrust to his ribs and a ridge-hand strike to the jugular, Nicki disabled him long enough to grab her charm.

He came back at her with the knife.

Four reverse punches in a row and several full-out kicks to his midriff rendered him powerless.

She leapt out to the platform.

There wasn't enough time to swing to the downspout, and it was too far to jump.

Phil was running up the alley. She had to get to the discs before he did.

She climbed over the metal rail, slid her hands down the rungs until they were almost at her ankles, and hung from the balcony. Then she let herself drop.

Nicki raced onto the subway and headed straight to Mac's residence room.

When she got there, the door was closed.

"Mac!" She banged it with her fist. "Mac, let me in." Nothing.

Oh, no.

"Mac! Mac! I know you're in there. I've got to speak to you. Please, Mac."

Still nothing.

"I was at Quon's tonight." There was no time for beating around the bush. Nicki was blunt. She lowered her voice and put her mouth right up to the crack in the door. "I know what you did, Mac, and I'm here to help." Nicki put her ear to the door and heard a moaning sound.

"Mac!" she cried.

Another student came out of his room when he heard her shout.

"What's going on?" he asked.

"I think Mac's in trouble. He's hurt. I need to get in there immediately."

"I'll get the hall supervisor. Hang on."

They had the door open within minutes.

When Nicki stepped in, Mac was lying on the floor along the side of his desk, his head pushed against the base of his chair.

Beside him was the bottle of painkillers.

And it was empty.

★　★　★

"It's not your fault, Margo," said Nicki. "You had no idea that Mac had a gambling problem."

"It wasn't up to me to give him those pills." Her face was streaked with red lines where the tears had stung her cheeks, and her body was limp. "I'm not a physician. Not even a pharmacist." Her bottom lip trembled uncontrollably. "Some nurse I am."

"Those were over-the-counter pills, Margo. Anyone can buy them, and in any amount." Nicki took her hand. "Nursing is a profession that has to be learned over a long period. By the time you finish your training, you'll be the best nurse in the city."

The charge nurse summoned the girls to her desk.

"They've pumped Mr. MacDonald's stomach. His tests don't show any brain damage, but the lining of his stomach is severely inflamed. He's weak, but he wants to see you both."

She looked at her watch. "It's late. But under the circum-
stances, I'll let you girls talk to Mr. MacDonald for a few
minutes. A *few* minutes. By the way, he'll be staying with us
for a few days."

"Why, are there complications?" Nicki asked the nurse.

"No, I don't believe so. But your friend shows signs of
stress-induced depression."

"I don't doubt it," said Nicki.

The girls sat with Mac for a while before Margo was called
away to help on another floor.

"Well, I guess I should thank you," said Mac, his voice so
weak it was almost a whisper.

"But you don't want to, because you wish I hadn't shown
up. You wish you'd been successful, right?"

Mac's silence said it all.

"I was at Quon's tonight, Mac. I know everything."

"What are you talking about?"

"I know he's a loan shark, I know he's using your gambling
addiction to control you, and I know he's forcing you to give up
technological secrets to the Chinese government."

Mac didn't respond for a full minute. Finally he spoke.

"Are you going to call the RCMP?" he asked.

"No. But I think *you* should."

"What, are you kidding me? And spend the rest of my
days locked up in a maximum security prison with nothing but
four walls and a wasted life to stare at?" Mac let his head drop
back onto the pillow.

"Why would you end up there?"

"You know why," he snapped.

"You mean for giving Quon the discs that had your professor's research on them?"

"Yes," he said quietly. The shame in his face was unbearable for her to look at any longer.

She put the envelope in his hand.

Mac was stunned. His jaw dropped.

He looked inside at the discs, then pressed the package against his chest. "I…I don't understand. How did you—?"

"It doesn't matter. The important thing is that you turn yourself in, Mac. It's the only way you'll be protected from Quon—he's out to get both of us now." She sighed. "And it will give you an opportunity to get some help for your addiction."

"You mean a few months in rehab?"

"Something like that."

"Does T'ai know any of this?" Mac's voice trailed off as he asked the question.

"No. It's up to you what you decide to tell him." She came closer to his bed. "Mac, I need you to be honest with me, okay?"

"For sure, for sure."

"Do you know anything about Dr. Aisin-Gioro's disappearance? Did you pass along any information about him to Quon?"

"No."

"Have you heard *anything* about a Ming vase?"

"Vase? No."

"Do you know anything about my friend, David Kahana? Is Quon the one who stabbed him?"

"Yin, I don't know. I swear to you." He propped himself up in the bed. "I am a compulsive gambler—I admit it now. And I am the top-ranked student in telecommunications engineering. Quon is working with spies from the People's Republic of China—and they are good at what they do. There's a million and one ways they could have found out how to get to me. And they did." He made a fist and tried to pound it into the bed beside him. "They did!"

"How do they find people like you?"

"By trolling chat rooms, intercepting cell phone calls, using back doors."

"Back doors?"

"Back doors in telecommunications equipment. They can monitor everything, believe me."

"That's wild," said Nicki.

"Manchurian microchips are central processing units, CPUs, that can be activated to allow the chips to "call home" and export information to the Chinese government," he explained.

"No way." Nicki leaned forward. "Why is it Manchurian?"

"The name comes from a movie, *The Manchurian Candidate*, in which a prisoner of war is implanted with a microchip. I suspect that's how they tracked down T'ai's uncle. Beijing's intelligence agencies must have hacked into his computer."

"You could be right," agreed Nicki. "And that's how they found out that David Kahana was meeting him to give him the Ming vase."

"What's with this vase?"

"It's a long story. Right now, you better get some rest. I shouldn't even be here."

"Yin," said Mac, "How am I supposed to make this up to you?"

"I'll think of something," she said. "But first—"

"I know. Call the RCMP. Or the Canadian Security Intelligence Service."

"I can bring an agent from CSIS over here tomorrow."

"How can you?" wondered Mac.

"I can."

"There's no reason to think they'll be lenient with me, you know. I have absolutely no proof that I was being blackmailed."

"Actually," said Nicki, "you do."

Chapter Nineteen

Nicki got up early the next morning to make time for a long run. When she returned, she found Fenwick preparing a full breakfast.

"It being Sunday," he said, "I took over for the cook."

Nicki noticed two places were set on the terrace.

"I didn't know my mother was home," she said.

"Yes, Miss. She arrived late last night." He gave Nicki a quick wink. "About an hour before you did. I took the liberty of telling her you'd retired for the night."

"Thanks for covering for me, Fenwick." She glanced at the clock. "I'm sorry about breakfast, but I've got to go. Soon I'll be able to sit down with you and enjoy all these great meals." She explained about Mac. "The croissants look terrific, by the way." She took two for the road.

"What shall I tell your mother?"

"Tell her I'll be here for dinner tonight. This time, I mean it."

Fenwick raised an eyebrow.

"I promise."

★　★　★

Nicki rapped lightly on Mac's door. "It's me. And I've brought someone along."

"Come in," he said.

"How are you, Mac?" asked Peter Byron.

"I'm, uh…okay. But what are you doing here?" He looked at Nicki. "I thought you were bringing…some other people."

"For such a brilliant guy, Mac, you can be pretty clueless," said Nicki. "Mr. Byron is a CSIS agent."

"What?" Mac pulled himself up, then hunkered down again when a sharp pain hit his stomach.

Nicki handed him a glass of water. "Sure you're up to this right now? We can come back later."

"I'm okay."

"Your friend here gave me a call," said Byron. "She knew that I'd been watching you." He sat down in a chair next to the bed and pulled another over for Nicki.

Byron took out his wallet and showed him his identification. "I guess you know I'm going to have the RCMP bring you in for questioning. You will be arrested."

Mac nodded, then gave Byron a full account of what he'd done.

"So you turned over the discs to Quon?"

"I did," admitted Mac. "But Yin got them back. I don't know how, but she did."

Byron turned to Nicki.

"Are you aware of what kind of a guy you're dealing with here? Quon will track you down. I guarantee it."

"I'm not afraid of Quon." She handed Byron her cell. "He'll be in jail soon, anyway."

Byron played a portion of what she'd taped.

"I'll have the RCMP arrest him today." He took another look at the video. "I've been after this guy for months now but didn't have enough proof to haul him in." He tucked the phone into the inner pocket of his jacket. "I do now."

"But what about Dr. Aisin-Gioro?" asked Nicki. "If you arrest Quon, how can we find out who he's working for? Without that information, we'll never locate the professor."

"We'll offer Quon a plea deal. He'll talk."

"And if he doesn't?"

"That's the chance we'll have to take."

Nicki wasn't about to take any chances.

"Suppose I tell you I know who Quon's working for, but I don't have any direct evidence?"

"I'm listening," said Byron.

Nicki sat down next to him. "The manager at Haddon Heights. Trent Newman."

Byron laughed out loud.

"What makes you say that?" he asked.

"A few things," said Nicki.

Byron continued to laugh.

Nicki became defensive. "Okay, a lot of things," she said. "Like erased surveillance footage and a Mandarin dictionary. And the fact that he tried to kill David Kahana a second time."

Byron was still smiling.

"What's so funny?" she asked.

"Newman is one of our agents."

"What?" cried Nicki.

"Yeah. He's been working on Quon's case with me for a while now."

Nicki was flattened. Embarrassed even. And it showed.

That's why Newman had Byron's e-mail address. How stupid of me!

"Look," said Byron, "I'm sorry. I didn't mean to offend you. You've done Newman's job for him, for heaven's sake. He'll be very pleased with the evidence you've collected. As I am." He patted his jacket pocket. "We'll replace your phone tomorrow."

Nicki got up to leave.

"See you later," she mumbled.

She opened the door and T'ai walked in. "Margo called me," he said. "She told me everything, Mac." Then he looked at Nicki. "You okay?" he asked.

She took off.

"Are you tired, Nicole?" Mrs. Haddon asked her daughter. "Have you been doing too much judo, dear?"

"I'm all right, Mother," replied Nicki. "And it's kung fu."
She pushed her dessert around on the plate.

"I can tell something's bothering you," said Mrs. Haddon.
"If it's about your friends at the delicatessen, I fixed that after
you called me in Hawaii."

"Thanks, Mother."

Mrs. Haddon summoned the maid to bring her another
cup of tea. Just as she'd finished pouring, Fenwick came into
the dining room to tell Nicki's mother that she had a call from
San Francisco.

"Tell whoever it is that I'll return the call shortly, Fenwick."

"Yes, Ma'am."

"So are you going to stay in Toronto, or are you return-
ing to Honolulu?" Nicki pulled her chair out from the table to
stretch her legs for a minute.

"I'll be here for a few days, then I'm meeting your father
in Rome. We're hoping to open a new location in Tuscany, but
we have to deal with the Italian government, of course. The
usual red tape."

Nicki nodded politely but hadn't heard a word her mother
had said. Her mind kept swinging back to Newman.

I don't care what Byron says. I don't trust that man.

"What do you think of the manager downtown?" she
asked her mother.

"Trent Newman? He's all right, I guess. Does his job."
Mrs. Haddon poured cream into her cup from a silver service.
"Why?"

"You don't have his job application kicking around, do you?"

"It's probably in my desk at the hotel," she replied.

"Do you know if he's a Canadian citizen?"

"Sure he is," her mother answered. "He was at our Vancouver location, before he came here." She thought for a second. "But he was born in the United States, I think."

"Let me guess. Honolulu, right?"

"I think so." She took a sip of tea. "Yes, I remember now. One of his references was from his days at the Pink Lady."

"The Royal Hawaiian Hotel?"

"Yes," said Mrs. Haddon. "It was years ago, but that's where he started out. As a bellhop, something like that."

Nicki shook her head.

"What's the matter, dear? Why do you care if he came from Hawaii?"

Fenwick interrupted.

"I'm sorry, Madam," he said. "But there's another call. This time it is…well, it's urgent. It seems there's a problem downtown."

"There is?" she said, getting up from her chair. "What kind of a problem?"

"I don't know, Ma'am. They didn't divulge that information to me."

"Oh, all right. I'll take it." Mrs. Haddon went to her study.

Nicki handed her plates to the maid and headed out onto the terrace. She watched clouds form in the sky. The Don River Valley was at its greenest at this point in the summer, especially before a thunderstorm when the colors of the forest stood out brilliantly against the dark gray background.

Nicki was deep in thought when the sound of the television through the screen door grabbed her attention.

The six o'clock news was under way, and the first story was the arrest of Quon. She ran inside and turned up the volume.

The RCMP have made an arrest as a result of a prolonged investigation into technological espionage activities involving several countries.

Quon's photo flashed on the screen.

More arrests are expected.

Nicki clicked off the television and returned to the terrace.

Fenwick followed her out. "Do you know something about the arrest?" he asked.

Mrs. Haddon slid back the glass doors and joined them outside.

"Nicole, that was the concierge at the hotel."

By the expression on her face, Nicki and Fenwick knew something was up. Something big.

"It's Trent Newman," she said. "He's disappeared."

Everything rushed into Nicki's head at once.

The vase.

T'ai's uncle.

Hawaii.

Newman's friend Kimo, the cop.

"Of course," she said under her breath.

"Of course?" Fenwick raised an eyebrow.

"Mother," said Nicki, "you were right when you said that something was bothering me."

"Oh?"

"I really should have stayed in Honolulu. I need to get back for an important…uh, competition…tomorrow afternoon. Do you think you could get the pilot to file a flight plan for me tonight? I know it's last minute, but this would mean the world to me."

Chapter Twenty

Nicki looked out across the blue Pacific. The flight above the island of Oahu, and the glorious birds-eye view it provided of Pearl Harbor and Diamond Head volcano, was always an exhilarating moment—especially as the plane descended over the pineapple fields and headed out onto the offshore runway, built on a coral reef.

This time was different. Nicki couldn't concentrate on anything, knowing what was about to unfold.

"I've got to go, Mother," said Nicki, "we're about to land. I just wanted to say I'm sorry for being such a jerk about the private jet. I'd be nowhere without it." She paused. "Or you."

She clicked off her phone.

The moment she landed, she thanked the pilot and took off to find a cab.

"Get me downtown as fast as you can," she told the driver. "Not the Nimitz Highway, I don't want the scenic route." She looked at her watch: it was still on Toronto time. "Take the H-1."

"You got it."

"What time is it?" she asked him.

"Nine twenty."

"Good," said Nicki, adjusting her watch back six hours. "The morning rush is past. We can do it in half an hour."

"Sounds like you've been to Honolulu before," said the driver, pulling the cab out of the terminal. He looked at her in his rearview mirror. "Don't I know you?"

"I don't think so. Listen, I've got to get to Beretania Street—to police headquarters."

"Okay. Fasten your seatbelt!"

The driver got her there in thirty-five minutes.

"Thanks," said Nicki, rushing to pay him.

"Would have done it in less than thirty if that moving van hadn't slowed me down," he replied, but Nicki was already in the front door of the building.

The Police Headquarters was a large four-story concrete structure with a front window like a tollbooth.

The receptionist put down her book.

"Yes?" she asked.

"I need to speak with an officer," said Nicki. "I'd like to talk to Lieutenant—"

"Wait here," she said, pointing to an uncomfortable bench and handing Nicki a plastic badge.

Five minutes passed before someone came. Nicki read his nametag anxiously, but it wasn't the cop she wanted.

"I'm sorry," said Nicki. "I was hoping to speak with a friend of mine."

"A friend?"

"Not a friend exactly, but we have a mutual acquaintance. Is Lieutenant Kimo...uh—"

"You mean Captain Kimo Moi." The officer headed back into the hallway. "I'll get him for you."

Thank goodness he's here.

While she waited, she pumped the receptionist for information. "So is it true that a replica of a Ming vase was stolen from the police museum down the hall?" she asked, hoping her suspicions were right.

"Yes," replied the woman. "Happened a few weeks ago. We still don't know who took it. Or why." She put down her pen. "It's not all that valuable."

"What's not valuable?" The brusque voice behind Nicki belonged to Kimo Moi, a tall man with an agitated face and huge sweat rings under his arms.

"The Ming vase replica," said Nicki.

"What did you want to see me about?"

"I need to talk to someone," she replied. "About the theft of the real one."

"Real what?"

"The real Ming vase."

He did a double take and then pulled her aside.

"Come in here," he said. He closed the door of the

interrogation room behind them. His eyes flashed. "What are you talking about?"

"Well, you see, I've been visiting some friends in Canada, and—"

"And?"

"And I discovered the identity of the person who took both the replica from the museum and the real vase, too. It was transferred to Toronto, to be given back to its rightful owner, but—"

"What are you talking about?"

"I was going to report this to the Toronto police, but I figured there was little they could do, now that the man who did this is here in Honolulu."

Silence.

Gotcha! thought Nicki. Then she continued.

"I'm going to find Mr. Newman now—that's his name, Mr. Trent Newman—but I didn't think it would be wise to confront him alone."

"No, it wouldn't," said Kimo Moi. "I'll take you there myself."

I thought you might.

"Do you know where he's staying?"

No, but you do, said Nicki to herself.

"I figured you could put out an APB and find him fairly quickly. Of course, I could always go to the FBI. They'll help—"

"No. I'll check my files. Maybe this man is on record."

Moi went away for a minute, pretended to check his computer, then returned with an address.

"He's likely in Manoa."

The captain told the receptionist to divert any calls to his assistant. Nicki followed him to the cruiser. His wheels screeched as he tore out of the lot.

He drove at high speed through the streets of Honolulu, running every red light he met. His hands gripped the steering wheel so tightly that his knuckles turned white.

The temperature rose quickly as the sun moved higher into the sky. Nicki went to open the window, but it was locked.

"Hot in here," she said.

He offered no reply and, with one angry flick, clicked on the air conditioning.

They sped past bus stops, markets, and homes with blooming lilies and mai-say-lan trees on their front lawns. Everything looked so normal, so peaceful.

Kimo Moi didn't say a word. He barreled eastward through the downtown core until he came to that part of Oahu where the urban core meets the greener outskirts and high-rise buildings begin to mix with old Japanese temples and monkeypod trees. Up and down the winding slopes of the Manoa Valley he careened, occasionally turning his head just enough to look at Nicki out of the corner of his eye.

She kept focused on what she had to do: she kept her muscles relaxed, her mind calm, and went over everything she'd learned in her years of training.

Action, not reaction.

If attacked, place yourself in a position of advantage while allowing your opponent to enter a position of disadvantage.

Moi made his way to a residential area. Spread across an overgrown green hillside was the old Chinese cemetery, where graves dated back to some of the earliest immigrants to cross the Pacific Ocean. It caught Nicki's eye, and she was momentarily deep in thought, until the police captain pulled his cruiser into a driveway and parked. Bougainvillea vines climbed up the high wooden fence that surrounded the house.

"He might be in here," he muttered.

Nicki followed him to the porch.

Every window shade was drawn.

He knocked once, then thrust open the door and threw her inside.

"What's going on?" came a voice from the next room. "I thought you were—"

Newman stopped dead when he saw Nicki standing there.

Moi closed the door and locked it.

"What the…?" Newman's eyes flew open, and his jaw dropped to the floor. "What's *she* doing here?"

"You know this girl?"

"She's a housekeeper. In Toronto. But—"

"Where is he?" Nicki demanded. "Where's the professor?" She ran into the kitchen, then the living room.

"Stop her!" hollered Newman.

She pulled open a door that led downstairs into a cellar.

"Don't go down there," screamed Moi.

She could hear the faint muffled sound of a man's voice. "I'm coming," she said, and started down.

Moi drew his gun. "Make one more move and I'll kill you."

Chapter Twenty-One

Nicki turned around slowly and came back up the stairs. Then she spoke to Newman directly.

"You'll be charged with the attempted murder of David Kahana, you know." She moved carefully, taking very small steps. She kept a conversation going with Newman, but never took her eyes off Moi. "Not to mention espionage."

"Who do you think you are?" said Newman. Then he looked at Moi. "I hired this kid a few days ago."

"I wish you hadn't." Moi kept the gun pointed at Nicki.

She spotted a large box with several layers of mailing tape wrapped around it.

"The vase. It's in there, isn't it?"

When they didn't reply, she continued. "I know you're a double agent, Mr. Newman—a mole for the People's Republic of China. You knew when Master Kahana would be alone at the school. You knew he was there to meet Professor Aisin-Gioro. You stabbed him, took the vase, and then put a phony in the safe in room 813 to cover your tracks.

"That replica," continued Nicki, "came from the Honolulu Police Department museum—it was a stand-in for the real one in the vault. Captain Moi here must have sent it to you."

She took a long, deep breath.

"I know that you are both working for Chinese Intelligence—it's the only way you could have known about the Ming being transferred. What I don't know is whether you confiscated the vase on orders from the Chinese government, or planned on disappearing with a fortune for yourselves. Either way, you had to make sure the professor never made it to Toronto. I guess you told him there'd been a change of plans and that he was to meet David Kahana here in Honolulu."

The two men exchanged glances.

"Do you have a silencer?" Newman asked the captain.

"Not here. We'll have to take her someplace," said Moi, and while he concentrated on answering Newman, Nicki pounced in a split second.

She delivered a mantis claw strike to Moi's face. When he raised his arm to stop her next blow, the gun dropped from his hand.

Newman reached for it. As he bent over, she directed every bit of force from her body to her hands and gave him a full throttle chop to the back of his neck.

Moi came toward her. Using the fireman's throw, so the

weight of his own body would be used against him, Nicki hurled him against the wall. A brass floor lamp fell on his head.

Newman came at her from behind.

She struck him with a back kick—a vicious move, used in the martial arts only for situations of extreme danger. Then, in full fighting stance, her legs positioned for balance and strength, she utilized a phenomenal twisting punch. With lightning speed, she delivered four kicks, one after the other, rendering Newman defenseless.

She grabbed the gun and ran downstairs to free Professor Aisin-Gioro.

He was on the floor in the middle of the room, bound and gagged. He was pale and barely conscious.

"I'm here to help," she said, quickly removing the cloth from his mouth and working hard to untie the heavy ropes around his ankles and wrists.

Upstairs, Newman and Moi were back on their feet. Moaning in pain, they stumbled to the top of the cellar stairs.

Nicki drew the gun.

"Back up or I'll shoot."

She tried to get Dr. Aisin-Gioro to his feet, but his limbs were too weak.

"Get your other gun," Newman hollered to Moi.

Nicki heard a cabinet bang shut, then steps across the floor. With an assault rifle under his arm, Moi returned to the top of the stairs. He loaded it, aimed it squarely at Nicki, and put his finger on the trigger.

Then came the voice she had been waiting for.

"Come out with your hands up. Don't make any sudden moves or we will shoot to kill."

The S.W.A.T. team surrounded the house.

Finally.

Glass smashed into a million tiny pieces when an officer kicked in the back door.

Newman and Moi tried to escape through the kitchen window, but it was too late.

"This is the FBI," came the voice from a police megaphone. "Surrender now. We're coming in." There was a brief pause, followed by a loud crash.

"Drop to the ground."

Nicki waited a few minutes and then hollered for help. "I have a man down here in need of immediate medical attention." Paramedics rushed into the cellar with a stretcher. They carefully lifted him onto it.

"I'll make sure one of the officers gets your vase, sir, and keeps it safe for you," said Nicki, leaning over the professor so he could hear her.

He nodded his head and lifted his hand slightly as the medics carried him out to a waiting ambulance. Nicki followed them outside. Dozens of specially trained officers, wearing full combat gear and carrying machine guns, had formed an impenetrable circle around Moi's house.

"Is he going to be okay?" Nicki asked the ambulance attendant.

"He's dehydrated and very weak, but I think he'll make it," he said.

Nicki walked over to the FBI investigator, special agent Kwai. "Has someone got the vase?" Nicki asked her.

"Here it comes now," she said. Another agent had already removed the tape and opened the box.

Nicki carefully lifted it out.

"Oh," she sighed, "it's gorgeous." She turned it from side to side slowly.

"What are you looking for?" asked Kwai.

"I want to see the scratch."

"The what?" asked Kwai.

"The imperfection."

Kwai didn't know what she was talking about.

"There it is!" said Nicki. "There's the scratch on the Ming vase." She pointed to a small score through the petal of a flower, a peony, made hundreds of years before.

"We'll take it to the field office for safe keeping." The officer held out her hands for the vase and then looked at Nicki. "Which is where I need you to go. We've got some people at the bureau who would like to meet you, Miss Haddon."

"Miss *Haddon*?" said Newman. "What! Are you kidding me?" Two agents had him in handcuffs.

"Get him out of here," said the investigator.

Newman glared threateningly at Nicki as they led him to a waiting van.

"I wouldn't worry about him," said Kwai. "With the charges he faces here and in Canada, he'll never make it out of jail. Not in this lifetime.

"I must admit," continued Kwai, "I had my doubts when

you called from the plane. But you were right—this was the best way to get Moi to show his hand." She raised an eyebrow. "When you told me you were working with Kahana, you didn't mention you were a teenager. You didn't mention MI6 either."

"The British Secret Service?" asked Nicki.

"Somebody there had your back. That's for sure."

Nicki watched as a group of people strolled through the Chinese cemetery across the street. "I'll just be a minute," she said.

Nicki headed down the slope. Headstones of all shapes and sizes were scattered haphazardly across the hillside. She made her way to the older section, where Hawaii's early settlers had been buried; years of backbreaking work cutting sugar cane and sandalwood had sent many of them to an early grave.

Her mind turned to her parents.

She wondered if they were still alive.

She wondered if they ever thought of her.

She wondered if she'd ever get to meet them.

Chapter Twenty-Two
One Week Later

"There's something I have to tell you, Nicki, but you must promise me that you won't let it influence your decision." David Kahana pushed his elbows into the bed to pull himself up. "Close the door, will you?" She did as he said, then he continued. "The best surgeons in the world can't help me now. I've lost the full use of my legs."

"You mean—"

"I'll be able to get around with a cane. And I might even be able to show you some hand-to-hand combat moves. But my days in the Secret Service are over, Nicki. From now on, my work will be in recruiting and training students I can count on. Like you."

"Oh, Master Kahana, you were so close—"

"I did make it. They've awarded me the title Supreme Grand Master."

She sat down next to him.

"I don't know what to say. About anything."

"You don't have to say anything. What I need you to do is consider my offer very carefully." His eyes moved to the doorway when someone knocked.

"Come in," he said.

It was Peter Byron.

"Good morning, David. The nurse told me you were accepting visitors." He looked at Nicki. "I guess an apology is in order."

Kahana responded for her.

"She's not one to gloat."

"I would if I were her," said Byron.

"In kung fu," explained Kahana, "the first thing you leave behind is your ego."

Nicki moved to the window and looked out at the streets of Toronto. "I don't mind that part. It's my friends I don't want to leave.

"I was just getting to know people here," she continued. "For the first time in my life, I have friends who care about me." She turned around. "I guess because they don't know who I am. If they did, well—"

"They'd love you just the same," said Kahana.

"Will I be able to say good-bye?"

"Yes, Nicki. But whatever your decision is, nothing we've discussed can leave this room. Not ever."

"Of course," she said.

"I've spoken with Officer Kwai from the Honolulu field office, and she's been in meetings all week with the top level FBI and CIA agents," said Kahana.

"And I'm here to remind you of your Canadian citizenship, Nicki." Byron sat down in the chair next to Kahana's bed. "I went to Ottawa yesterday, and I met with the head of the Canadian Security Intelligence Service."

"Does he agree?" asked Kahana.

"Yes. CSIS realizes that the time has come for action. Foreign spies have stolen considerable business and industrial secrets from this country, and yet we have no agents working in other countries to stop this activity before it happens. The organization believes that offense may be the only defense.

"The problem," he continued, "is that we have no facilities to train agents for this kind of work. Not the way the United States and Great Britain have."

"So, I'd be training in the United States?"

Kahana answered the question.

"First with MI6 in England and then with the CIA in the States. And when you finish, you'll be Canada's first foreign operative, providing intelligence to all three countries."

"But I thought the Secret Service wanted computer experts, people like that."

"They do. But not in the field," answered Kahana.

"Too dangerous?" she asked.

"In a word," he said, "yes."

"What do I tell my parents?"

"We'll look after that," said Kahana. "We'll set things up so they think you're attending a school in the United Kingdom for the martial arts. And that you have to leave immediately."

"I don't know," said Nicki.

"What don't you know?"

"Can I ask you something, Grand Master?"

He nodded.

"How do you justify lying to people? If there's one thing I've learned from my years of training in martial arts, it's the importance of honesty."

Kahana thought for a minute. Then he answered.

"If you're true to yourself, and if you follow your heart, then everything you do will come from the right place. It will be right."

Nicki understood.

She reached for the door handle, then stopped. "There are other elite athletes in the world. Why me?"

Then, answering her own question, she said, "Because I'm female, I know my way around virtually every city on the planet, I have wealthy parents, and most important of all, because I am Chinese."

"Because you are an exceptional athlete, you are bright, you are intelligent, and, above all, you are brave." Kahana smiled. "I rest my case."

Then his expression changed.

"Of course, Nicki, the decision must be yours."

Chapter Twenty-Three

"Where shall we put it, Lila?" asked Nicki. "How about over there, next to those figurines and bowls?"

Nicki moved the vase to an upper shelf near the back of the store.

"No way," said Lila. "I want it in the window. It'll draw in the crowds. I can tell them all about my brother-in-law's Ming." She wrote *Not For Sale* on a card, then taped it onto the vase.

"You mean you aren't going to sell this? I figured—"

"What? That I'd try to pass it off as the real thing?" She made a face. "Now would I do something like that?"

T'ai laughed.

"She figures it'll make everything in here look a shade better."

He carried in a tray of sandwiches and cookies and pink lemonade.

"Girls like pink lemonade, right?"

"Right," said Nicki. "Everything must be pink, T'ai. The pinker the better." She winked at Lila.

He poured everyone a glass, then raised his hand to toast his friend. "To Yin!"

"To Yin," said Lila, and they all clinked glasses.

"Thanks, but I'm just glad your uncle is back home and doing well," replied Nicki.

"You were right about Newman. Thank goodness you were able to alert the authorities in Honolulu in time. I still can't figure out how you put it all together."

Lila looked at Nicki. "She's psychic. Like me."

Nicki smiled. "Does your uncle have his vase back yet?" she asked.

"Came and went," said Lila.

"What?" asked Nicki.

T'ai explained. "My uncle never wanted the Ming for himself. He's just glad it didn't wind up in the wrong hands." He took a drink of lemonade. "He's donated it to the National Museum of Art in Beijing, as a gift from the descendants of the former royal family. That way, it will be enjoyed by everyone."

"And maybe they'll learn something about the Cultural Revolution," added Lila. "It was no picnic for the family."

Nicki nodded. "I hope he can find a way to return to China one day," she said.

"Maybe that angel of his will help him," declared Lila.

"Angel?" asked Nicki.

"He claims that when he was unconscious, nearly dead, a Chinese girl came to his rescue. The FBI insists there was no such girl, that she was a figment of his imagination. So he figures she must have been an angel." T'ai laughed. "Crazy or what?"

The three of them spent the lunch hour sitting outside the store, watching people as they strolled by. When a group of tourists came along, Nicki left them so they could make some sales.

"See you soon!" said T'ai, heading inside with Lila.

Nicki watched them for a minute and wondered about her own grandparents. *I must have a grandmother someplace. Maybe she's like Lila.*

"See you," she said.

She looked up at the sign that said *One-of-a-Kind Finds* and smiled.

I hope so.

I really hope so.

Next she went to the deli. The supper crowd hadn't arrived yet, so she had a chance to talk with Margo.

"You girls sit down for a while," said Mrs. Bloom. "We can handle things."

"Thanks, Mom," said Margo. "So where have you been, Yin? I haven't seen you all week!" She pulled napkins out of the dispenser and gave them each one. "There were a couple of women from the hotel here yesterday, and when I asked about you, they said you'd left!"

"Oh, Ellen and Dolores. How are they doing?"

"They both seemed very happy—celebrating something. I think they got a raise."

"It's hard work they do," declared Nicki. "I'm going to try something else for a while." She pulled in her chair. "How has business been here?"

"Not bad," replied Margo. "But the really great news is that the Haddons have offered us a long lease. With no rent increases!" Her eyes lit up. "Did you hear about Mac?"

"T'ai told me he's not going to have to spend any time in jail. So that's good."

"It sure is," agreed Margo. "He has to go to Gamblers Anonymous meetings and talk to high school students about addictions, but he'll be able to finish his studies."

"Here you are, girls," said Ira, his voice booming across the deli. "Cheesecake." He clunked down a giant slab in front of each of them. "Coffee?"

"Fill it up!" said Nicki. "You've trained me to like this stuff, Margo."

The girls laughed and talked, and Margo told Nicki all about what she'd been doing at the hospital, the new patients, and her plans for the school year.

"You really enjoy your work, don't you?" Nicki asked.

"I do," said Margo. "It feels good to know I'm making a difference. A small one, maybe, but at least it's something."

Before they knew it, it was almost four o'clock, and Margo had to start preparing meals.

"Guess I'd better get back there and help my folks," she said.

Nicki waited for the kitchen door to swing shut behind Margo, then headed to the cash register. She checked to make sure the customers were engaged in their conversations and not watching what she was doing.

I love this place, she thought. *I'm so glad they're going to be able to stay.*

Then she reached for the honeymoon jar. Inside it she put two first-class, round-trip tickets to Hawaii.

She was almost out the door when Margo called to her.

"Drop by soon!"

"I will, Margo," said Nicki.

She went to leave, then turned around.

"Margo—"

"Yeah?"

"Take care of yourself, okay?"

Epilogue

Nicki found her seat on flight 427 to Heathrow airport and waited for the other passengers to board. She rested her elbow on the edge of the window and watched as jetliners flew in and out of Pearson International Airport.

Her thoughts turned to David Kahana and the instructions he had given her. She was to board the plane and wait to be met by a British Secret Service agent, who would travel with her to London and let her know where she'd be staying after that.

It wasn't until everyone had taken their places aboard the aircraft that she felt someone sit down next to her. Without shifting her gaze from the action on the tarmac, she greeted the person beside her.

"Hello, Fenwick," she said.

There was silence for a moment.

"You knew?"

Nicki turned and smiled at him. "From the minute you let me sit in the front seat of the limo, I realized that you were no ordinary butler."

"I see."

"There's one thing I'd like to know, though," she asked him.

"What's that, Nicki?"

"How did MI6 find out about me?"

"From watching you compete in Britain." The butler fastened his seat belt.

"Where will I be living in London, Fenwick?" she asked. "Near the hotel?"

"Not in London, Nicki," he replied. "You could be recognized. You'll be staying in Milchester, with my sister Emma."

"Milchester?"

The jet's engines roared.

The plane was getting ready to take off.

Nicki looked out the window as the plane taxied across the tarmac and took its position on the strip. It moved faster, faster, faster down the runway.

She felt for her good luck charm and cupped it in her left hand.

"Weren't you surprised when they told you I had consented to all of this?" asked Nicki.

"Not really," said Fenwick. "I know why you accepted the position."

She looked down at the charm.

"It's because of them, isn't it?" he asked.

The jet climbed into the cloudless sky, up and over the skyscrapers of Toronto. Within seconds, the city below became a checkerboard of colors—the cars and the people nothing but tiny specks on the face of a giant jigsaw puzzle.

"If it takes the rest of my life," said Nicki, "I'm going to find my parents. Wherever they are."

About the Author

Caroline Stellings is an award-winning author and illustrator. Her book *The Contest,* part of the Gutsy Girl series, won the 2009 ForeWord Book of the Year Award and was a finalist for the 2010/11 Hackmatack prize. Besides her many books for children and young adults, she is also the writer of *The Nancy Drew Crookbook*, a long running series in *The Sleuth* magazine. She lives in Waterdown, Ontario.